Dale Stromberg

MELANCHOLIC PARABLES

Being for the *antiselving* reader

Petaling Jaya

Published at *considerable* expense
and with much *bother* and *ado*
by the author himself.

This is probably a work of fiction. All of the characters and events portrayed in these parables are either products of the author's imagination or are used fictitiously, probably.

MELANCHOLIC PARABLES.

Copyright © 2022 by Dale Stromberg.
All rights reserved. No wrongs reversed.

If you wish to use any part of this work for a purpose normally restricted by copyright, contact the author. *Fair use* is specifically encouraged and is to be interpreted broadly. The author also welcomes anyone who has paid for a copy of this book to *share* it with whomever they like.

Published by Dale Stromberg
Petaling Jaya, Selangor, Malaysia

dalestromberg.jimdofree.com
twitter.com/StrombergLit

Cover design © 2023 by Rachel A. Rosen.
https://rachelrosen.ca/

Typeset in Ten Oldstyle and Helvetica Neue.

To the Reader

You, there. Perhaps you are wondering whether this collection of parables is right for you. Perhaps it is not.

Not every book is for every reader. A book must rhyme with you, or you with it. I suspect this book is for antiselving readers. What does it mean to antiself? Though I cannot explain, allow me to explain:

Consider this assertion: *I don't exist—I happen*. That is, suppose *self* is an act which is convinced it is I.

Suppose, in other words, that *self* is not a noun but a verb: *to self*.

Now, some verbs can be negated in two ways:

> ☞ The sun *rises*.
>   1) The sun *does not rise*.
>   2) The sun *sets*.
>
> ☞ The door *opens*.
>   1) The door *does not open*.
>   2) The door *closes*.
>
> ☞ The sky *brightens*.
>   1) The sky *does not brighten*.
>   2) The sky *darkens*.

Consider the possibility that *self* can also be negated in two ways. *Not to self* would simply be not to happen. But suppose another antonym of *to self* is *to antiself*.

If *to self* meant to rise,
                to open,
                    to brighten,
then *to antiself* would mean to set,
                      to close,
                          to darken.

Suppose you were to antiself. Who would happen then?

Would that person shrink from the succor of human company, joining the absurd kith of the lonesome, ill at ease to be known of, melancholic and unsuited to selving?

If so, then perhaps they will find these parables to rhyme with the antonym they are.

∾

☞ You may find content warnings listed in the *Schedule of Parables* on page 176.

THE FIRST THIRTEENTH

Autumn on Venus

Dree Your Weird

*Learn to love disappointment
as the ear loves a resolving chord.*

Hello. Welcome. Step right in, sir.

Yes. No, not a pet, sir. I am the proprietor.

I assure you, yes. Not a joke. Owner and operator, sir.

Not a cow, sir. A bull. The difference? Ahem. I'm surprised you ask.

Yes, right this way. We stock dinnerware, toasting flutes, vases. Christmas ornaments along that wall. Tumblers of every variety by the window displays.

Oh!

Oh, dreadfully sorry. I've just—well, yes, it seems every time I turn around, this sort of thing—no, really, I'll clean it up myself.

I beg your pardon? Well... yes. The—the merchandise. We do carry quite a bit of... shall I say, weathered merchandise?

Well, I suppose, yes. Broken, sir. Strictly speaking.

No, sir, what you see is what we have.

Well. I can hardly deny it when you put it so plainly, but... yes. Indeed. Not surprising at all, being that I am a, as you say, sir, yes: a bull.

Is it really so amusing, sir?

Well, please do come again. You won't be? I am sorry to hear it, sir.

Open a what instead, sir? Ahem. It is the, erm, female of the species that gives milk, sir. But I thank you for the suggestion.

Good day, sir.

Albumen Skyline

Serenity: learning what to fear.

Let me tell you what I know of Bellatrix Sakakino. She works for an auditing firm, is thirty-two years old, and is unmarried. Half-Japanese, half-Danish. Former avid hiker. Also, her body has a dampening effect on nearby electricity.

This power is involuntary. She'd rather be rid of it, if only she could. Simply imagine the inconvenience.

Suppose yourself walking through, say, Sangenjaya at night, glancing furtively at the faces of passersby, peering furtively into shop windows. Bright lamps line the streets here; the stars, even if you looked furtively up at them, would scarcely be visible.

Upon turning a certain corner, you come to a street with but a few solitary walkers. The lamps here stand at farther intervals. In every sense, this street is less lively. Ahead, you see a dark patch.

She's there, moving in your direction.

As she approaches each street lamp, its light gradually dims. At just the moment she passes, it is entirely extinguished. As she moves beyond, it slowly rekindles. Her posture, her gait, the direction of her gaze, all are indistinct to you in the gloom surrounding her.

In this way, her eerie shroud of black draws ever nearer. An atavistic fear seizes you. Your feet become leaden; you slow to a standstill beneath a street lamp.

Bellatrix and her enveloping darkness come upon you. The street lamp dims and dies.

Your terror peaks in the instant she passes—but you feel an overpowering urge to glance furtively at her face in profile. You cannot.

Instead, not knowing where to look, you turn your gaze up to the sky. It is bespangled with meek and tranquil stars.

Ngantukisme

*A superpower common to all social animals: invisibility.
To vanish, be alone.*

You were strolling to the supermarket. A person walking in front of you fell to the sidewalk. You checked her pulse; she wasn't dead. Just sleeping.

All around you, people began teetering. Falling asleep on their feet. Cars rolled aimlessly to a halt. Some bumped into the curb.

At the supermarket, customers and stockers and cashiers draped over each other in the aisles. With no better idea of what to do, you left money by one of the cash registers and carried your groceries home.

Turned on the news. The anchor was asleep at her desk. The camera angle was funny too.

Turned the faucet handle, but no water came out. Then the power died. Glanced at your phone: no service. Walked outside to see what was happening, but from every open window came the sound of snoring.

"Oh, for heaven's sake," you thought, as within you there bloomed a sick and helpless envy.

Et sic per gradus ad ima tenditur

You're so very kind; I can scarcely bear it.

When Bellatrix Sakakino died, her ghost was received by low-voiced figures in lustrous robes who said, "Welcome to your golden moment."

The warmly lit room had a timeless, restrained elegance; the only furnishings were a walnut chaise longue and a bell cord to summon aid. In this place, the most perfect moment of Bellatrix's life was preserved, its every detail precisely captured. She was to exist inside it forever.

A robed figure gestured to her to be seated.

Light shimmered as though a curtain were parting, and there she was again—the Kyoto International School Academic Olympiad awards ceremony. She'd nearly swept the categories when she was twelve, surprising no one more than herself. Now, as though translated bodily into that twelve-year-old self, she saw, heard, and even smelled it exactly as she had then: the tidy rows of folding chairs, the cheery squeak of sneaker soles on the inlaid linoleum floor, the pine scent of the janitor's detergent. Her mom sat beaming in the front row, mobile phone stowed in her handbag. On the auditorium stage in front of the entire seventh grade, Mr. Pearson hung three gold medals around Bellatrix's neck: Mathematics, Public Speaking, and Spelling. Her heart was fit to burst. On a giddy whim, she leant in toward Mr. Pearson's lapel mic and repeated a joke she'd heard from television: "I just want to thank all the little people." It got a laugh. Never again would she be so happy.

She returned to herself in the chaise longue in the afterworld, swelling with the same fullness of spirit, the same rare and fleeting joy of feeling she really mattered. Then it began again. Bella lived this ambrosial experience over and over. Hundreds, then thousands of times, each a perfect reiteration of the last. That happiness was to be hers for all infinity.

Then she began to notice, within the blissful repetition, a tiny flaw. It was a small point—trivial, really—but that "little people" joke just wasn't quite perfect.

Like a pebble in a shoe, what began as a petty distraction grew to be irritating, then intolerable. The joke was trite. People must have been laughing at her, not with her. Condescending to an ugly *hāfu* girl who thought she was being clever. Or laughing nervously in embarrassment for her, the obliviously awkward girl, the peg who stuck out, the one who, practically every day of her life but this one, did nothing but offend, annoy, or discomfit others. As the myriad unfriendly eyes weighed her, even the files of metal chairs seemed to stand in judgmental ranks against her. The shrill squeals of shoes on linoleum set her teeth on edge. The pong of the janitor's detergent failed to mask the moldy musk that plagued the auditorium. Still she couldn't stop telling and retelling the joke. And who were the "little people"? Her friends? Her mom, who took so much time off work to support Bella's studies and activities that it cost her a promotion to line producer? Did her mother's smile tighten slightly, being called "little" like that? In the unalterable memory, Bella wasn't looking in the right direction—she could never quite see her mother's face.

At last, it got to be too much. If she had to live inside a golden moment for all eternity, any other would be better than this. Bellatrix stood from the chaise longue, pulled the bell cord, and

Autumn on Venus | 9

summoned the figures in robes. "Is heaven always the same?" she complained. "Does it never, ever change?"

The figures in robes shook their heads. "No, Bellatrix," they answered. "Heaven is always different."

A New Lease on Life (with No Escape Clause)

I have strong opinions, not strong convictions—
so I hate myself for doing what I hate myself for doing.

Bellatrix Sakakino was reborn with all the memories of her previous life intact.

She solved algebra problems while still in diapers and corrected her mother's grammar before her milk teeth were in. Toilet-trained herself as soon as physiologically possible. Didn't merely sing along with nursery songs—sang in contrapuntal harmony. Parents and educators were astonished. They also found her disquieting.

Kindergarten was much less confusing the second time around. When Jimmy McDaniel called her "Smellatrix" and blew fart noises at her, she recognized it as merely an attempt to gain approval from their peers at her expense; the giggling didn't bother her. Being more mentally and emotionally mature than her classmates, she never made friends, and never wanted to.

Still, she erred.

One morning, she pointed out to her kindergarten teacher—a kindly fellow, though she could scarcely believe he'd finished high school—a factual error in his Safety Rules poster concerning whether pencil lead contained actual lead. All the mothers were there for observation day. Poor Mr. Bell looked like he might choke. Bella realized it would have been better to bring it up in private.

That afternoon, when Owen Adebayo, a bashful, docile child, had a strawberry Go-Gurt that Bella coveted, she convinced him to split it. She figured she knew how to handle child psychology: with enough ten-cent words and projected authority, before long she had him *wanting* to share. At the end of recess, she saw Owen sobbing alone by the playground backstop. The murmur of her better nature came, as always, too late.

After school, her mother surprised her with a pricy Sylvanian doll. Bella, hoping to avoid conflict, lied sweetly and said she loved it. So her mother went out a week later and bought a whole collection of them, planning to delight her. There was so much else the money could have been spent on; Bella found herself unable to playact the requisite joy. Mommy was crestfallen.

Each time, Bellatrix felt the smart of conscience ever more sharply. And with a prior lifetime's worth of mistakes also in memory, the weight of living grew heavier and heavier.

What a peculiar child she made.

White Hat Bias

*Truth: the balancing point between credibility
and the cost of being wrong.*

Leigh, a furniture designer, was devoted more to the creative side of her work than to the pecuniary details. Her staff included a full-time accountant, coincidentally named Lee, who tracked the company's financial health. Freed to focus on what she loved, Leigh applied herself to her drafting table and workbench.

Leigh's designs were good. Minimalist, innovative. But not always commercially viable.

Right from the start, Leigh and Lee shared a remarkable connection. When Leigh turned her ankle on an uneven spot in the parking lot, Lee limped for a day afterward. After Lee had radishes at lunch, Leigh was gassy and kept having to excuse herself from meetings. One Saturday, as Leigh watched *Grave of the Fireflies* alone in her apartment, Lee, alone in his apartment, had a good cry.

Given this connection, it was natural enough that Lee would quietly fall in love with his boss. He wanted more than anything to make her happy; her happiness, he felt, would be his. Sales dropped off, and the company descended into the red, but he began to falsify data in his reports to her, counterfeiting financial viability. His intent was not to deceive her but to spare her from pain.

But finally, the company's fortunes sank so low that it could not remain operational. His sadness made heavier by the weight of months of deception, Lee prepared a final, entirely truthful financial report for Leigh. His meeting with her was arranged for the following morning; he was awake all night fretting over how she would take the shock. Leigh also slept poorly, though she did not know why.

The next morning, as Leigh was en route to the meeting, an oncoming car crossed the centerline. She was killed on impact. Since she died ignorant of the truth, one might say Leigh died happy.

And Lee, waiting in her office, died in the same instant. Also happy.

The Martyr's Palm

Paper-based billing, unlike automatic bank transfer, compels one to decide whether to do what one must.

At the supermarket, only two cash registers are operating. After evaluating the customers and cashiers, trying to guess which line will move faster, Bellatrix Sakakino tentatively chooses the one on the right.

Is the world mist? she wonders. *Or am I the mist?*

She remembers his hands. His elbows. His substantial shoulders.

If I'm only proud of myself when I'm quiet, why can I never stay quiet?

His skin smelled like tobacco. His breath at night was irregular and turbulent.

Am I doing the same old thing for a brand new reason?

She has come to buy milk—that's her pretext, anyway. The walk from her apartment was refreshing. The year is just warming.

Does another person's shame give me the right to behave shamefully?

She likes her neighborhood. It's a quaint street, a mix of tiny shops and modest homes. It all has to end.

Should I hate him? Am I in love with being in love? Is self-destruction really so romantic?

The year will run out. Winter always comes back. And she's going to leave this neighborhood. She *wants* to—it's a great comfort to plan to leave.

Am I just a pocket of lukewarm air?

Sometimes the least painful way to leave somebody is for them to leave you.

Do people really mingle souls together?

A look at the other cashier's line shows that it's moving faster than hers. Which gives her a moment longer.

I never have.

THE SECOND THIRTEENTH

Burglar's Wine

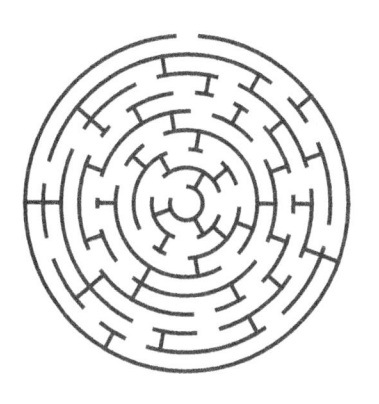

We Drink Pearls—We Sup on Peacocks' Tongues

You're human if:
  a) you can't understand why not everyone is human.
  b) you can't understand that not everyone is human.

The other day, I went to a smoke concert. It was *fantastic*.

The band came out on stage and took their positions. At stage left was the pipist. They started with a country number, so he was smoking a corn-cob.

The two cigarists were at stage right. The rhythm cigarist stood near the back, while the lead cigarist was out front, smoking passionately.

The rhythm section was at rear center stage. There was a calabash pipist, a hookah player, and a multi-smoker who alternated between a calumet, a sebsi, and, for ballads, unfiltered cigarettes.

Of course, the star of the show was the frontwoman, who stood at the lip of the stage with her foot up on a monitor, head to toe in black leather, blowing mentholated smoke rings.

The whole band smoked and smoked like gangbusters. Not a sound was to be heard. It wasn't long before the air was so thick that nobody could even see the stage.

The crowd went *wild*.

Þanne Ytemeste Ferþyng

> *Good on purpose: +5 points*
> *Good by accident: +2 points*
> *Evil by accident: −5 points*
> *Evil on purpose: −5 points*

Around lunchtime, when the lettuce in her salad begins to curl and brown beneath her fingers, Bellatrix Sakakino notices that she has become radioactive.

The coworker at the next table in the break room casts odd glances at her, then suddenly clutches his forehead—he has mutated, forming a third eye.

On the subway home, she triggers more mutations. A dozing businessman on the seat across from her scratches his nose with a six-fingered hand. A young mother nearby gasps—from within her baby buggy, a scaly tentacle snakes out.

After that, people around her start dropping dead.

Bellatrix is captured by radiation-suited police and taken to a government facility. Doctors behind thick glass use robot arms to test and probe her.

They hypothesize that the source of the radiation is something on her, perhaps something she's wearing. Is it coming from her overcoat? They strip it off of her and test it.

No, it's not the overcoat.

Nor is it coming from her clothing. Not her shoes or handbag. Not her undergarments. They test for some sort of radioactive dust on her skin, but it's not that either. It's coming from within. Killing everyone around her. Leaving unharmed only Bellatrix herself.

At that moment, an even fiercer wave of radiation flashes out of her, and the doctors behind the glass are burnt to curling ash and crumble away. Alarm bells ring and sirens wail, but, apart from Bellatrix, there is no one to hear them.

Endlessly Cutting the Deck

Gave up. Continued to hope anyway.

What if you could go back in time to take a peek at the life of someone who would go on to change the world? Would you want a chance to see them when they were still an unknown, when no one around them might yet suspect their future significance?

Would you like to peer through the schoolhouse window to see Einstein as a child, figuring sums? What if you could sidle close enough to hear him thinking aloud under his breath?

Would you like to disguise yourself as a merchant or laborer in seventeenth-century Latvia, there to catch occasional glimpses of the humble child who will grow to become Catherine, empress of Russia?

Imagine placing yourself in just the right spot on a street corner or busy marketplace, where you will opportunely bump shoulders with a yet-unknown Oprah Winfrey, Benjamin Disraeli, Toyotomi Hideyoshi, George Eliot or Andrew Carnegie.

In the future, this will be possible. Time-travel tourism—going back to spy on the famous before they were famous—will develop from a curiosity to a boutique industry to an enormously popular leisure activity.

Floods of people will pay handsomely to be transported into the past, outfitted with period-accurate clothing, and placed strategically to get a look at a future giant of history. Of course, there will be strict rules against interacting or interfering. We can't have clumsy tourists changing the future on us. They only look—they never speak, never touch.

So ask yourself: Do you sometimes feel watched? Do you sometimes sense the eyes of strangers on you?

Might this explain it?

Excellent Problem-Causing and Critical-Drinking Skills

Hardly anything is as selfish as self-sabotage.

"What are you smiling about, scumbag?"

They tied you to a board and whipped you. They yanked your fingernails out with pliers. They burnt you with iron pokers.

They put electrodes on your privates. They dunked you in water till you choked. They kept you hooded all hours.

They locked you in a box three quarters your standing height, too narrow to sit. They beat you with rubber hoses. They sliced off a nipple.

"What are you smiling about, scumbag?" they demanded.

"Right now," you replied, "it's *all about me*."

It Is One Hundred Years since Our Children Left

You hide your pain behind your back—we only see its shadow.

Bellatrix Sakakino perpetually craved her favorite food. Her problem was that it was a rather unconventional favorite. The food she loved most of all was the fruit of the Nilgiri holly.

Though their dull pinkish hue was unexceptional beside the lascivious black of cherries or the lucent green of juice-pregnant grapes, the very thought of the berries filled her with a longing she could no more explain than subdue. She needed them. They were necessary to life as she understood it.

What was wrong with that? First of all, Nilgiri holly fruit was slightly toxic to humans. When ingested, it induced vomiting and diarrhœa. A proper bellyful would guarantee her a trip to the emergency room for a dose of activated charcoal.

But no matter what she ate, nor how much, Bellatrix was never satisfied. No meat, fruit, vegetable, cheese, legume, bread, grain or drink hit the spot for her. Her only hope of satisfaction was the Nilgiri holly berry. The craving began even before she could remember. It was as if she were born desiring *this* fruit above all others.

Of course, she had never tasted it. The Nilgiri holly went extinct in 1859, more than a century before she was born.

Life with Good Demons

Virtue in extremity breeds harm.

A genie comes out of my lamp and promises me three wishes. "Wish now."

"End all wars," I command.

"Done," quotes the genie.

In the distance, I hear the firing stop. One last bomb bursts in air, probably shot off just before the cease-fire.

"Redistribute all wealth," I command.

"Done," quotes the genie.

In the distance, I can hear ninety-nine voices caroling, "Hooray!" One voice mutters, "Aww, crud."

"Let love reign," I command.

"Done," quotes the genie.

In the distance, a bomb bursts in air. The guns open fire. A single voice shouts, "Woo hoo!" and ninety-nine mutter, "Crud."

In despair, I demand, "What went wrong?"

The genie chuckles through her nose.

My Teeth Floated Out of My Mouth

The problem with my excessive self-love:
Though you tell me how wonderful I am,
I simply cannot accept it.

Bellatrix Sakakino used to live for the screams of the crowd. She'd take up her stance at center-stage, everything still dark – a single spotlight would hit her – the band would rip into the opening chords – and that's when it would happen. The screams!

In Japanese, they call those screams *yellow voices*. Why yellow? Bellatrix had no idea. But there was nothing in the world like it.

It nevertheless startled the hell out of her the first time she heard yellow voices during sound check. No crowds, just musicians and venue staff. Her band played a verse and chorus to check levels, and when it ended—a frenzied ovation. It sounded like the entire Budokan cheering, though the seats were still empty. "Enough with the horse shit," she said sourly to the sound guy. She assumed he was playing yellow voice clips through the PA.

It was even less amusing when she started hearing yellow voices at band practice. The guys claimed they couldn't hear anything. The instant a song ended, the same deluge of rapturous screams rushed upon her.

She'd shut all the windows of her condo before strumming work-in-progress numbers. Still, the yellow voices would seep in. Out in the street, she saw only passersby.

She quit singing in the shower. Quit humming under her breath as she jogged around Inokashira Park. Would kick herself if, preoccupied, she unconsciously whistled a bar of something. Longed for escape, for relief.

The constant adulation—it felt unbearably insulting.

THE THIRD THIRTEENTH
Chewing Your Cremains

Tumpangisme

Give me liberty, or give us death.
(Says Jephthah, too low for his daughter to hear.)

Tried swallowing poison. Tried swallowing mousetraps. Tried quicklime, helium, eye of newt, flea collars, fragments of naugahyde, a mysterious fish doll, a cabinet key, and sand. Began to despair of ever being cured.

So then, nearly at the end of my rope, I swallowed an eraser. It was a white, gummy one, and it tasted like an eraser. Soft as a berry but too, too dry. It wasted no time, but got to erasing straight off.

Gone were my tumors. Gone, polyps. Gone, swelling and bloating and abscesses and plaque. Gone, hateful tapeworm. I tell you, I felt like dancing.

But then it erased my appendix. I should've been more alarmed than I was. But you know what they say about the appendix.

It got my large intestine. Gouts of eraser shavings came up, burp after burp. I began to feel nervous. My small intestine didn't last much longer, and then it erased my stomach and my liver. Pancreas, gone. Kidneys, gone. I started to worry about my lungs, and about my spleen and bladder too.

About my heart, I wasn't so worried.

I had to do something to plug the dike, and I had to act fast. I swallowed you. I opened my jaws impossibly wide, like a python or a baleen whale, and down the hatch you went. What was my plan? Well, don't laugh, but I thought you'd be my eraser-stopper. I thought I'd figure out the details once you were down there.

How was I to know the eraser would erase you too?

It has already rubbed away your entire left leg. Parts of the fingers on both hands. Your crow's feet and the mole by your belly button. Both eyebrows. I imagine you look perpetually surprised now. With no eyebrows, that is.

Once it erases you entirely, I don't know what I'll do.

Holocutor

She left a trail like a meteor. He was merely the sky.

You're out floating in the ocean. It's a terrible storm. The wind snatches foam from the whitecaps.

A great wave lifts you and dashes you against the rocks on the coast. The ebb sweeps you back out to sea. This happens again and again.

The rocks are sharp and cruel. The waves are powerful and violent. The wind never relents.

Your smile is wide. Your eyes are shining. The pleasure is unbearable.

Privatspheric Pressure

Water: wash thyself.
Leaf: shade thyself.
Wind: cool thyself.
Thou: know thyself.

Bellatrix Sakakino has another contrevoyant dream. A totally cute one this time.

She's a spunky wee hedgehog, always in a tiff. What color is she? Well, why not pink? Pink is cute.

"Could you give me a hug? Please? Pretty please? A hug?" she walks around demanding, cute and pink and prickly. But nobody offers to hug her.

When everybody rejects her, she goes off into an even stormier tiff, and her spines stand up still taller and pricklier.

"How come nobody wants to give me a hug? How come? How come?"

Right to the end of the dream, she's all by her lonesome.

Just before she awakes, somebody, exasperated at her grousing, asks her, "So when's the last time you gave a hug to another hedgehog?"

Never, she realizes.

Se Unclæna Gast

Make people forget their problems
by obliging them to rescue you from your problems.

You used your finger to draw a circle in the sand about one meter across, then rimmed it with runes. Pricked your thumb with a needle.

Then you summoned me. I appeared—flash of light, whirl of smoke.

The bloodlust of the undead upon me, I lunged for you. But your runes and incantations hemmed me in. I couldn't escape the circle.

I raged, spat foam, demanded release, swore to rend you limb from limb. It was no use.

In thunderous tones, I demanded to know why you'd summoned me from my long sojourn through arid places. I swore eternal hatred.

But I *could not escape the circle*, and this fact—it gave me great relief.

Your runes bestilled me. I knew you'd never free me. You were safe, so I was safe.

Insolubilia

Ninety-nine bottles of ire on the wall.
Ninety-nine bottles of ire.
We take one down. Pass it around.
How many bottles are left on the wall?
(I can't bear to count. Because there are ninety-nine.)

Bellatrix Sakakino and her boyfriend Amrish had a fight. They *had* it, the way you have a baby.

Fights grow up fast. Before long, their fight was old enough to have fights of its own. It had two.

Each of those two soon had two more fights, and each of those soon had two of their own. And on and on.

While human parents generally die before their children, one peculiarity of fights is that they can only die after their children.

And they don't move out of the house.

Farewell to the Anthropocene

I sent Bellatrix Sakakino a thesis: "$1 + 1 - 1 = 1$?"
She replied as I guessed she would: "$0 + 0 - 0 = 0$."

According to data released today by astrophysicists from the Sloan Digital Sky Survey, the Earth is slowly but steadily moving away from the Sun. Findings indicate that an ever-deepening cold will grip the planet, which is projected to become a lifeless, icebound mass in three to five years.

We must watch this happen: our crops will die beneath snowfall out of season, our populations panic and riot, our numbers dwindle. Our generation is the last. All our noise and passion, our going and getting and doing, must slow and stop. The story of our kind will never thereafter be known.

The question is, why must this come to pass?

Has the Sun's gravitational force weakened, like a lover who, the heat of his passion dissipating with time, no longer pulls his beloved nearer?

Or is the Earth drawing away, like a daughter grown to womanhood who rebels against her parents, asserting herself, testing her freedom?

Or is the Sun pushing us away, like a husband whose love has abruptly turned to hate and who fervently desires never to see his wife again?

Disconcordance

*The sadness of being unseen,
and the keener sadness of being seen through.*

I peeled my shadow from the floor and wadded it into a ball. "Ready?"

Bellatrix held her hands out to catch it. From me to her, it was maybe three meters.

I wound up. Smiled shyly. "*Sure* you're ready?"

"Just throw it, stupid."

I threw it.

But in mid-flight, my shadow stalled—not heavy enough, defeated by drag. Began to unfurl in midair. Plopped onto the floor between us, well short of Bellatrix's outstretched hands.

The look on Bella's face—I'd seen it before. And the tired sigh. The unsurprised, contemptuous sigh. I'd earned it, I supposed.

But it broke my heart.

THE FOURTH THIRTEENTH

Punchline to the Apocalypse

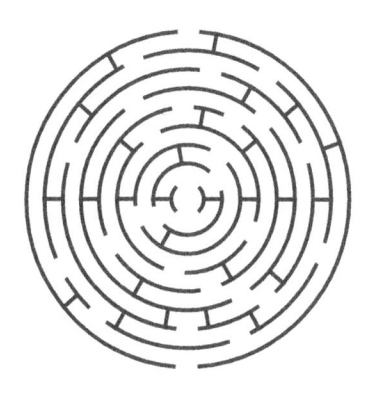

Brain, Brain, Go Away

If I were beautiful when I cried,
I would find occasion to cry.

I brush my teeth with shampoo. I wash my face with vegetable oil.

I comb my hair with a pencil. I put the baby to bed in the washing machine.

I sprinkle sawdust on my spaghetti. I send email to my bookshelf.

I play my violin with a dishrag. I feed deodorant to my rabbits.

I alphabetize my spoons. I peel potatoes with pliers.

But it all feels wrong.

Dryshod on the Waterface

A great thinker's fear: to be held responsible for her followers.

Bellatrix Sakakino read about the Turing Test on the internet: if a human asks a machine a sufficient number of questions, and cannot tell from the answers whether it's a machine talking, then the machine is deemed intelligent.

She immediately grasped the potential of using this test to evaluate whether *other* forms of intelligence existed.

To establish a baseline, she began by subjecting her brother Sinclair to the Turing Test.

(It behooves us to mention that Sinclair had, for years, been sick to death of Bellatrix. He'd learned that, when one of these tomfool notions gripped her, the only intelligent response was stony silence.)

For five minutes, Bellatrix peppered him with random questions. His response: stony silence. She carefully recorded this response in her notebook.

Her next test subject was a smooth round stone from the garden, selected for its pleasing shape and texture. It responded to her questions exactly as Sinclair had done. This also she recorded.

After this, she subjected the Deity to the same set of questions. When comparing her notes on the three subjects' responses, she was astonished to find that they were, not merely similar, but identical.

This was good enough for her. She immediately converted to animism.

Gardener of Human Happiness

—Why did you enslave us?
—Because my love of liberty is tameless.

In a dusty old cookbook, Bellatrix Sakakino found a recipe titled *The Perfect Omelet*. Intrigued, she copied it out and took it to work.

"Let's make this," she said to her kitchen staff.

The opening paragraph of the recipe read, "This omelet will not merely be good. It will be *infinitely* good."

It went on to say, "All that is required is the *will* to make the omelet. To stop at nothing."

"That's me," thought Bellatrix. "I have that will. I *feel* how true this is."

So she gave the kitchen staff an order: "Start breaking eggs."

"How many?" they asked her.

Bellatrix checked the recipe. It didn't say how many eggs she'd need to break. "Just—keep breaking them. We'll know we've broken enough when the omelet is made."

After the staff had broken tens of thousands of eggs, but the omelet had nevertheless not yet been made, one turned to another and muttered, "Seems an awful waste of eggs."

Bellatrix overheard. Enraged, she had the woman fired. Fired and shot. And her family shot. And her house burnt and leveled. And her name stricken from all public records.

"You either believe or you don't," she warned the others.

Burning of Judas

1. The Devil got my:
   a) stock options
   b) recumbent bicycle
   c) golf swing
   d) no-bid contract

Bellatrix at the bakery: tray in one hand, tongs in the other, picking out the bread she wants. This bakery isn't cheap, but the prices feel worth it since she's doing some of the work herself.

She gets two cheese-stuffed garlic rolls and a blackcurrant brioche. Goes to the register.

"Sorry, wait. No." Bellatrix gestures curtly to the girl in the too-precious kerchief—management probably makes her wear it. The girl was just putting the bread into a paper bag. "Separately, please."

The girl starts to wrap each item in its own sheet of paper. "No," says Bellatrix. "Break them up, please."

The girl breaks the bread into small pieces. "Smaller," says Bellatrix.

The girl breaks the pieces into smaller pieces. "Smaller yet," says Bellatrix.

The girl mashes and shreds the bread into numberless crumbs. "Good," says Bellatrix. "Paper, please."

The girl opens a drawer beside the cash register and brings out a box of tiny paper envelopes, each no larger than a postage stamp. Each crumb of bread goes into an envelope, which the girl licks and seals meticulously. The line of waiting customers behind Bellatrix grows longer and longer.

These paper envelopes go into larger waxed paper envelopes. Ten paper envelopes to one waxed paper envelope.

The waxed paper envelopes go into sealable plastic baggies. Ten waxed paper envelopes to one sealable plastic baggie. All this Bellatrix watches with luxuriating contentment.

The plastic baggies all go into a large paper bag. The girl in the kerchief tapes up the paper bag. Then, because it is raining today, she wraps the paper bag in a clear vinyl bag, presumably waterproof, and tapes this up as well. This parcel goes into a smart carrying bag with string handles.

Bellatrix receives this bag with an air of unsurpassed satisfaction. She strides from the bakery like a gambler who has just fleeced the house.

Persona bajo la lluvia

My best-loved poem: the dictionary.
A cornucopia of internal rhyme.

The myriad secrets that slink on the far side of postboxes, wardrobes, or phone booths... The phantasies and notions that live in the corners of our eyes, sliding away like a mote on the cornea... The djinns, kobolds, and paradoxes crowding behind each blade of grass... The secrets concealed just there, on the opposite face of the visible...

The world we see is merely a silhouette through paper, a faint hint of the hidden totality. This have I always known, and this have I dedicated myself to proving. It was in pursuit of my desire to see behind everything that I invented my shadow-detector.

This device makes use of a range of sensitive, carefully calibrated instruments—a luminiferosity gauge, an æther dosimeter, a Wakefield-Crohn tube, et cetera—in order to detect whether a shadow exists on the opposite side of an object.

Say you are standing to the east of a tree. Point the device at it, and the instruments will tell you whether the west-facing side of the tree is in shadow. Simple in principle; devilishly tricky in practice. In order to banish shadows from the front face of the object, allowing a more accurate reading of its rear and thus eliminating false-positives (the bane of scientific study), I also mounted a 500-watt quartz iodine lamp on the nose of the detector.

You will surely be astonished at my findings. I would choose a test object: a sofa, a vase, a parking meter, or a row of shrubs. I would visually verify, from multiple angles, that there was no shadow behind it. Then I'd fire up the detector and point it at the object. And I'd get a positive reading every single time.

It turns out there are indeed shadows on the other side of everywhere. We simply fail to perceive them—a sad human limitation.

Droll Tin Pannikins

Avoid repeating yourself by repeating someone else.

Bellatrix Sakakino isn't weight-conscious, not exactly. It would be more accurate to call her belt-conscious.

If her waist is just so slim, a certain hole on her belt will fit perfectly. If she thickens round the middle a given amount, the next hole up will be just right.

However, if she's between those two waist sizes, neither hole matches. So Bellatrix painstakingly gains or loses weight to make her waist size match the holes in her belt.

A new belt would mean a whole new diet plan.

Eia, wärn wir da!

*Utopianism: changing the world because
you cannot change yourself.*

Bellatrix Sakakino on her tribulations and persecutions:

"I wanted to open a bank account, but I couldn't find the lid. I wanted to hang up my mobile phone, but I couldn't find the hook. I wanted to hold a meeting, but I couldn't find the handle.

"I tried to turn on the record player, but it broke when I stepped on it. I tried to put out a fire, but it was too hot to carry. I tried to bring up my children, but no one wanted to talk about them.

"I wish I could play Mozart, but I never learned the rules. I wish I could fire my housekeeper, but I can't find her trigger. I'm also concerned she wouldn't give my house back.

"Why," she dolefully laments, "is this world so *fundamentally* imperfect?"

THE FIFTH THIRTEENTH
Good Morning Turnkey

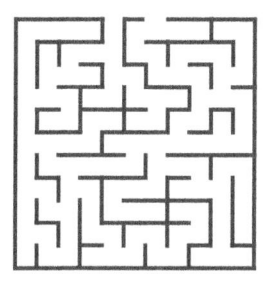

Fortnight of New Moons

*The self on Tuesday is prisoner to
the self on Monday—and vice versa.*

I was born a slave, in a castle where time had stopped. I still live here now. My job is to keep the place tidy.

The scullery wench sits motionless at her churn. The footmen outside the grand bedroom stand stock-still. Even the dew on the windows remains as it has been since before I was born, suspended in place trickling down the panes.

Inside the grand bedroom, the Beauty sleeps. My mother was a slave to Her, and only my mother remained moving when time stopped for the rest. That was fifteen years ago, just before I was born. Mother chose death last year.

There's not much for me to do. No one to tidy up after. I wish my mother had left just one cobweb, not swept them all away in her first week—of course, they never came back. Just to have one cobweb, to look at, to plan for. Perhaps to sweep away just before I die. It would feel like an accomplishment to wait that long.

The Beauty will sleep for a hundred years before the Prince arrives to kiss Her. At least, that was the story my mother told me.

Will I be here to see it? I suppose not.

My Memoirs Won't Mention You

*To inflict so much sorrow on others, only
by being selfish—how astonishing.*

Kali the Destroyer calls me up. "We're not going to do anything, okay? I just want to talk."

"Fine," I say. There's a knock at the door. That was quick.

Kali lets herself in and lobs a severed human head into the kitchen sink, then uses my dish rag to wipe her blood-smeared scimitar before dropping it onto the counter with a clatter.

"You know," she says wearily, "people assume I don't have feelings."

"Douchebags," I say sympathetically. I decide to brew us some tea. While the water boils, I sneak looks at her. She's fiddling absent-mindedly with her girdle of human hands. She looks fierce, full of beautiful black hatred. Her brow is wet; perhaps she's come straight from someplace tropical. "Tough day at work?"

She tosses her head irascibly and sweat droplets scatter, some transforming into Thuggees, who skulk away. "Oh, god."

"What is it?"

"Nothing." She stalks off to the only other room of my apartment.

I carry two mugs to where Kali has sat on the tatami floor, knees to her chest. When she doesn't take the mug from me, I place it beside her. "So, I want to hear about it, okay?" She doesn't answer. "I can't know if you don't tell me."

Good Morning Turnkey | 53

"Oh, so you *could* know if I *did* tell you?" She bites the words short. "You think *you're* lonesome? You don't know what lonesome is. Oh, god."

I take a stab. "Things not going too great with Shiva?"

She clucks and sticks her tongue out at me. "That faggot. Perpetually ithyphallic, and he never even *sees* me."

"He won't let you step on him anymore?"

"As if."

"There's other guys out there, you know." I don't venture to say who.

"I just can't." She runs her hand through her unbridled, matted hair. "It has to be him."

That's about what I'd figured.

"But I just wish…" She blinks her bloodshot eyes, and a solitary tear inches down her cheek.

"If only I could help." And here I am with my ulterior motives. I nearly disgust myself.

Kali turns to look at my face, gazing for a moment at me, into me, through me. Finally she speaks in her cold, cold voice. "Lie down."

I strip off my shirt and lie on my stomach on the floor, arms folded beneath my face. She straddles me and puts her hands on my back, beginning to rub hard, in widening circles.

Then she reaches her slim, gentle hands through the skin of my back and caresses and soothes me from within. Reaches down to my stomach and finds the black hole there and closes it up, and I'm further soothed. Reaches to my heart and plucks it like a pear.

I begin to fade away like a lightbulb on a dimmer switch. Fading and fading, finding relief. Mind and memory loosening. I cannot even recall what we were talking about a moment ago. Soon there is only my attenuating self.

My cheek against my forearm, I glance up to see her lovely frown, her erotic rage, her piercing eyes, as she bites into my heart, blood lapping down her chin, and then I fade all the way out.

Murmurs in the Moiré

Given the right crack, we'd all gladly fall through.

Sarah can't woolgather all afternoon. When she finishes dusting Abe's book cabinet, the oriental rug in the living room will be waiting for her to beat it. When that's done, the sofa covers will be waiting for her to strip off and launder them. When that's done, the parquet floors will be waiting for her to vacuum and dry-mop.

Her arms are folded, her hip canted against the love seat. No one ever tells her to clean this, clean that. It just needs doing. She stands looking out of the wide living room window. Audacious blue summer sky. Straight-sided lawns. But she can't woolgather all afternoon.

Garage door opener grumbles. Car engine pulls in, dies. Suspension creaks. One door slams, then another. Door from garage to kitchen humphs open.

"Have fun?" she calls, though she doesn't know where they went, doesn't know what for, didn't know when they'd be back. "I said, have fun?" Abe, silent, walks straight to the den, nudges the door shut with his knee. One of his solemn moods.

"Have fun?" she repeats to Isaac, who comes in after his dad.

Her son shrugs, mopey as ever. "Not really."

"Where'd you go?"

"Nowhere," he mopes.

Sarah sets down the dust rag on the arm of the rocker. "What'd you guys do?"

"Nothing. Just sacrificed a ram." Isaac glides mopily off to his room.

Sarah sighs slowly. *Sacrifice*—weird thing to say. They must have gone for mutton curry or something. But she can't woolgather all afternoon. The oriental rug waits for her to beat it.

Whilst This Machine Is to Him

The trouble with talking to myself: all the interruptions.

My dad was a woodcutter by trade, a jokester by disposition. He never met a bad pun he didn't like.

If he found us some fruit in the forest, he'd ask, "Orange you hungry?" If he killed a bear and wanted my help to lug the carcass, he'd say, "Can't bear it alone." If he was holding a box, he'd pretend to thump me with it and say, "C'mon, wanna box?"

The neighborhood witch had some sort of quarrel with him. I never understood why. She cursed his ax.

One day, the ax cut off his right arm. We had a replacement arm made out of tin.

When the ax cut off his other arm, all we could do was get him a second tin one. Should have thrown away the ax at that point.

It wasn't long before the ax had cut off each and every flesh-and-blood part of his body, even his head. He was all tin in the end.

He never let it get him down, though. He'd still pretend to thump me with a box and say, "C'mon, wanna box?"

And I'd smile. "Same old dad," I'd say.

Well.

Another thing that never changed was, my dad liked to sit in this one chair by the fire after a long day of work. It was his favor-

Good Morning Turnkey | 57

ite chair before he got chopped up, and it was his favorite chair after.

Now, my uncle wasn't a woodcutter like my dad; he was a mad scientist. He'd save each chopped-off bit of my dad, but he'd never tell us what for.

After my dad was all tin, my uncle stitched together all the old meat-and-bones parts of him, then jazzed them with a bolt of lightning. They came back to life.

My meat-and-bones dad relished corny jokes as much as ever. If I made him chuckle, he'd say, "I'm in stitches." His nickname for my mad scientist uncle was Body Builder. That sort of stuff.

But my meat dad and my tin dad didn't joke together much. In fact, they bickered constantly—especially over the chair by the fire.

"Get out of that chair," my tin dad would grouse. "It's *my* chair."

"No, it isn't," my meat dad would insist. "It's *mine*."

What Average Opinion Expects
Average Opinion to Be

*Flying first class: a tacit admission that you're not rich
enough to buy your own plane. How humiliating.*

Apollo's lament:

"I personally don't get it. Jehovah never wrote a poem, and Jesus never shot an arrow, far as I know. You never hear anybody praising Allah's good looks. What have they got that I haven't?

"So I decided to give it one more try.

"When I assumed human form, it wasn't to chase tail. That's my dad's deal—bulls and swans and shit. I set my sights higher.

"It's all about trends. Catching the right wave. Now, you look at modern human society, and it's obvious: *entertainers* are the suns at the heart of everybody's universe.

"Being, you know, the deity who inspired deathless paeans and epic poetry, I figured I'd lay waste to the songwriting game. I moved to Burbank and started making connections.

"I don't even need to ask—*of course* you've heard of my work. How about 'All the Saddest Girls'? Yep, thirty weeks at the top of the Hot 100. Or 'No to the Power of Yes', which Adele and John Legend both covered? Or maybe, I don't know, a little tune called 'Dreams of Gibraltar'? Yeah, the one Spielberg used in the movie of the same name.

"A hundred and fifty top ten numbers in a single decade—sixty-seven number one hits—so many gold records, you could melt them and build a statue. Take that, Paul motherfucking

Good Morning Turnkey | 59

McCartney. They've featured my songs at the Super Bowl, the Oscars—even the Olympics, which makes perfect sense, if you think about it.

"And you know what? Nobody's impressed.

"You've read that *Pitchfork* piece, right? I'll admit, I've got it memorized. Crap like this:

> Another impeccable Apollo album drops, and this very peccable critic yawns. No surprises here: the hired-gun singers turn in flawless performances, and the chords and melodies are so expertly balanced, you'll never—you cannot—get sick of them. Which is what I'm sick of.
>
> It'll sell millions. And?
>
> Never before has music so beloved been crafted by a musician this meh. Pop generated by Holy Algorithm may make hearts resonate like church bells, but this has translated into zero fan warmth toward the god himself. Is it any wonder? Remember *that smirk*? The meme that broke the internet when he swept the Grammys (again) last year?
>
> No struggle, no triumph, no conquering of personal demons. So Apollo has made Bob Dylan his bitch—so what? Dylan's music isn't perfect, but it's authentic. Lived in. Earned.
>
> Whereas for this smug twit, by default it's a cinch.

"And so on. Eight hundred words of bile, crowned with a relish-the-irony five-star rating. The review itself did *not* break the internet, but it got likes.

"Likes.

"I never used to let the haters bother me. Aesop once wrote a fable about a fox and some sour grapes; it so happens I inspired it for him. The haters should read it some time.

"But these days, it's just—it's gotten harder.

"A little *personal* recognition would be nice. One of those lifetime achievement awards. Or, you know, a fan letter. Because, damn it, I didn't get into the game to make hearts resonate like church bells. It's not my *music* I need people to worship.

"So—why? Why can't I catch a wave here?"

Lies Breathed Through Silver

It's better to be wrong than to learn you are wrong.

Poor old Geppetto was at his wits' end.

From the window, he could see the boy throwing his knife into the chestnut tree in the yard. Practicing his throw. Geppetto sighed deeply. "What pains this one has given me!" Not a day went by that they didn't argue.

There was the thieving. The fighting. The unsavory acquaintances.

There were the immoral girls hanging about—but who did Geppetto think he was fooling? Not one of them had been "immoral" before Pinocchio had got to them!

There were the insults. Worst of all, the insults! From his own boy! "Baldy. Homo. Butterfingers!"

Geppetto sucked back tears. "To be called a butterfingers by the boy I carved. Carved from wood with these fingers!"

The boy hadn't seen the inside of a school in years. He slunk around billiard halls, card parlors, opium dens—God knew where else.

As for work? Helping around the house? Oh, excuse me! Geppetto buried his head in his hands.

It seemed no father had ever been as miserable as he.

But the boy? Shall we ask him for his story?

Well, his schoolmates were cruel, naturally. There was the boy who patted a wooden playground bench and quipped, "Pinocchio's mom, so *supportive*." Soft cheeks burning with shame, Pinocchio would come home hoping to unburden himself, only to find Papa sunk to his knees. Always praying.

The time came when, if Pinocchio stuck his knife into a tree and some ass made a "matricide" crack, it would earn him a broken arm. Pinocchio stopped interrupting Geppetto's prayers with questions, never asking the one that burned deepest: "How come you never whittled me a mom?"

But the old man was whittling something or other. Sequestered in his work shed, windows shuttered. Pinocchio peeked inside once when Papa was sleeping. Once and never again.

So what if he yelled at the old crybaby? "*You* are the strings that hold me down." It felt good to let it out. "I liked you better when you could see I was lying." This was the closest Pinocchio got to saying what he felt—if he even knew what he felt.

Do we really want to ask Pinocchio all this? What would he tell us of disappointment in others? Of disillusionment at moral feebleness? The constant praying. The melodramatic sighing—the old man sounded like an affronted primo uomo. The maudlin need to be loved, loved, loved.

And the work shed. Pinocchio hated it. He could never unsee what he saw the one time he peeked inside: row upon row of new wooden boy dolls. Each looking just like Pinocchio before his miraculous transformation.

Maybe Geppetto never stopped whittling little boys, hoping for another good fairy to animate them... Or hoping the good fairy would *not* animate them... Maybe it wasn't God he was praying to night and day...

So, let's not ask Pinocchio. I think we'd rather not know.

World Turns to Slurry

To love your neighbor as yourself seems pretty heartless.

Narcissus's yew bow has a hefty draw, and few can boast the strength to bend it. But when he steps noiselessly into the glade and spies a roe deer, her nose to the pool, the bow arcs lithely as a reed. The hissing shaft buries itself in the unhappy creature's neck. The beast falls.

In this moment, this thrill like no other, Narcissus forgets all else. Thoughts and memories he can otherwise never escape slip away. And we, who know his looming fate, shall allow him this moment of relief.

He forgets the reproofs of his nymph mother: that he should have pitied Echo, who loved him so. *I couldn't answer her feelings,* he always insisted. *Wasn't it best to spurn her?*

He likewise does not think on the warnings of his river god father: that it was dangerous to be too beautiful. Narcissus's wonted retort was that he never sought, and had no power to diminish, his physical perfection. And his father would frown and mutter, *Of all men, your self-love is most justified—but have a care, son.*

Now, in truth, Narcissus has never loved himself any more than you or I do. No one in Thespiae can know it, but an inky dew has settled heavily onto the petals of his heart, weighing them till they droop beneath the load. The hunt is but a fleeting respite from the gloom crowding his vision, from the dispiriting conviction that to give himself to all who love him would be to betray each in turn—so that he is wicked whatever he does. He could not prevent Echo from wasting away, but this does not matter. He is guilty. Revenge is the prerogative of the gods, and someday it will come.

He hastens to the pool's edge to collect his kill, binding its legs with cord so he might hoist it onto his shoulders. The soft dancing tips of the water glint invitingly. He has been hours at the hunt; he is thirsty.

You know as well as I how this will end. Aphrodite will enrapture him with his own image. The pull of his bewitchment will kill him; the intensity of his unwanted beauty will overthrow him, trap and doom him as it did to Echo. He will bend to the pool to kiss his reflection and drown.

That is how it will appear to us. But not to him.

Crouching to drink, Narcissus catches sight of the loveliest face he has ever seen. He is not interested; beauty, he knows, is false. He turns his head away.

Except that he cannot. His muscles disobey him. His flesh crawls as a realization dawns: *I am not free.*

As though pressed from above, he sinks to the earth, to his hands and knees, and his face is drawn irresistibly to the water's surface. He sees carnage reflected on the wavering mirror. The arrow through the doe's flesh. An overturned chariot, the driver's neck broken beneath the crossbar. The earth after a battle, burdened with loathsome carrion.

Such sights—do we enjoy them? Narcissus sickens, but cannot look away; after all, it is only his own repulsive face he sees. And this bewitchment is nothing new; he has suffered from it for many a year.

Echo was my fault. There it is—the inner whisper. It comes often at night, when the coals in the brazier burn dim, when sleep stands off from him. *She would breathe still if I had never lived.* His iniquity rises before him to blot out the stars. Nothing else fits in his view.

I am wretched to the core.

How many times has he taken his flensing knife in hand and pressed the edge of the metal to his wrist, or his neck? How many hours have passed in which he could think of nothing but his own unfitness to exist? He would banish such thoughts, if only he could. But they come.

Did the gods curse me? he wonders, forlorn, right before the fatal pool claims him. *Or am I myself the curse?*

All he has ever managed to achieve, all he delights in, all those who mean more to him than he can ever mean to himself—these fade away. He sees only his own hateful form within the deep black water. This is the reflection he has no choice but to kiss.

THE SIXTH THIRTEENTH

Beware the Rope's End

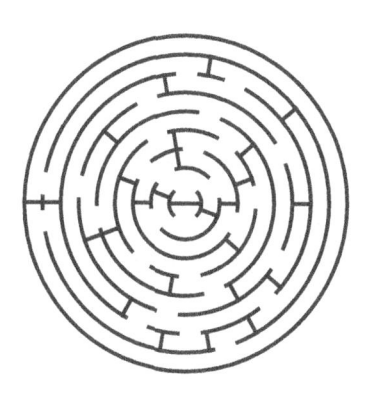

Obstrepolice

*The soldier killed for what he never stood for—
pity him?*

Things are going well with Bellatrix Sakakino's new boyfriend, Takuma, until he starts to show a weird side. It turns out he only eats or drinks things that begin with a vowel.

Udon or *oolong tea* are permissible. *Ramen* or *black tea* are out of the question.

Where it gets knotty is that, while Takuma can eat an *omelet* in English, the same thing in Japanese is *tamagoyaki*, meaning he can't touch it in that language. Dietary restrictions based on what language you're eating in can be the most nettlesome kind.

Why does this cause Bellatrix such problems? Because she can read plain as anything, in the wrinkle between his brows and the hesitation on his lips, that he hopes she will do likewise.

And how could she disappoint him? He's everything to her. She has no choice but to pretend to agree.

Care for a Canoodle?

*Our love might be so easily healed
if only you'd become someone else.*

You answer the phone—the landline; the one nobody ever calls—and it's a woman's voice, one you don't recognize. "Do you—do you have a girlfriend?"

Of course you don't. "Sorry?"

"I just—would you ever feel like maybe going out with me?"

"Um, who is this?" You can't place the voice. It's a voice that could be any age, but then again you decide it sounds young. Young and maybe cute. Cute and maybe pretty.

"I got your number from a friend," she says. "You're into hip hop, right?"

"Yeah."

"Me too. You like strawberry *daifuku*, right?"

"Yeah."

"Me too. Your favorite movie was *300*, right?"

"Yeah."

"Me too. You like it a little freaky, right?"

You cough.

"Me too! We're perfect for each other. I know this is out of the blue, but can we meet tonight? Or do you already have plans?"

Of course you don't. "Yeah, that is... out of the blue."

"In thirty minutes, in front of Hachiko in Shibuya. Okay?" Her voice is maddeningly alluring.

But Hachiko is always mobbed with people. "Um, like, I don't actually know what you look like."

"That's fine. You'll see me right away. I'll be the one with a vacuum cleaner. Okay? See you soon!" She hangs up.

Thirty minutes! You throw on some clean clothes, sprinkle on a bit of the cologne your mother gave you for your last birthday, and rummage through the drawer for a condom. You put it in your shirt pocket. No, make that your wallet. No, you decide the shirt is better. Got to go!

You make it to Hachiko and look around at the girls there. Cute ones, elegant ones, pretty ones, sexy ones. For some reason, Shibuya is wall-to-wall babes today. However, each and every one of them is dragging, pushing, or carrying a vacuum cleaner.

Come to think of it, you saw this on the news, didn't you? *Sōji-kyūto*: the latest trend "sweeping" Japan.

Your heart sinks.

Welcome and Heeded Prophets

*A couple trading hand signals,
an arch look, a mouthed oops.*

Bellatrix's cat, Blixa, naps on her thigh as she reads a magazine. His weight on her is calming.

As she folds the corner of a page, she unconsciously shifts her body a bit. Blixa mews once and steps lightly off her leg. He finds a spot to sleep at the other end of the duvet.

Bellatrix wants his weight again. But she can't just lift him and return him to her; she wants him not to *be* back, but to *come* back.

But she moved, so he moved. That's how he is.

Her phone buzzes. Another text. She knows who it is from.

Tant pis

Love: wanting to die in my sleep the day before you leave me.

Bellatrix Sakakino, as a child, trusted her mother—absolutely, implicitly. Her mother trusted her as well, but less. This is natural. Children will fib, or err, or fail to understand.

Bellatrix's first boyfriend, a magazine editor called Irvine, loved her with all the precipitousness of an emotional dreamer. She returned the feeling to a degree, but not entirely. She knew their relationship would have an expiry date; he only thought he knew this.

When Bellatrix moved from Fukushima to Tokyo, she left behind Minori, a bosom friend, and for a full year missed her terribly. They'd survived high school bullying together. Minori missed Bella as well, but less—she had other friends to resort to.

It was always this way. Bellatrix and one other person would sit in the scales; the one whose feelings were stronger would fall; the other would rise. Whoever fell suffered more.

Whatever Will Bain't, Will Bain't

Couples walk here of an evening.
"I was half of a couple once,"
thinks someone's wife.

Bellatrix Sakakino has become a mouse. In a wide, high-ceilinged house, as she scurries about in search of food, she watches for the cat.

Bellatrix lives in mortal fear of the cat. If it caught her, she'd be finished. Its curved claws would pierce her body, its powerful jaws would crush her, its merciless teeth would tear her, and her life would escape on gouts of blood.

The cat is many times larger than she, and many times stronger. Its body curves gracefully. Its sea-green eyes are lucid and mysterious, its movements quick and adroit.

Bellatrix both fears the cat and is drawn to it in trembling admiration. In a way, she loves it. *I wish I had been born such a glorious animal*, she thinks. *Notice me*, she silently calls. *I'm here. I've been watching you. Look at me.*

But what is this, suicide? Is she mad? Will she go to the cat and expose herself to it?

Bellatrix plucks up her courage and ventures out of her hole in the wall, step by tentative step, looking around all the while. Her tiny heart pounds. There, atop a tall shelf—the cat. Of course, it has spotted her with its keen eyes. It watches languidly. Bellatrix scarcely dares to breathe.

But the cat doesn't pounce. It looks at her for a moment more, yawns, and shuts its eyes for a nap.

Amorous Echolalia

First baby was an accident.
Got married in a rush.
Now they can't have another.

My right eye said to my left, "You and I were meant to be together. We're two of a kind. The ideal match. I just can't picture life without you. We think the same. We *move* the same. Promise you'll never abandon me. I couldn't face it if you left."

My left eye said to my right, "Look, it's over." It didn't say, "Let's see other people," or, "I need space to gain perspective." It said, "I'm done with you. I don't see it working out; I can't be lashed to you like this. You're not right for me. Sorry."

So my right eye spent the whole night crying. My left eye was dry-eyed.

Motif f388

*You've loved empty rooms ever since
you learnt to walk out of them.*

Bellatrix has gone from asking Tatsuya to make love every night, to twice or thrice a week, to once a month at most. She finds it increasingly difficult to enjoy sex with him—she knows she loves it more than he. For her, it's completion; for him, mere euphoria.

Tatsuya, who used to sing flamenco at the Fox and Goose open mic on Wednesdays, has given it up. It was painful to do, but necessary. For him, each note trembled with *tener duende*; but what shone in his listeners' eyes was, not bewitchment, but plain delight.

Isolde opened the Fox and Goose after years as a chef, but her staff prepares the bar food. Though all agreed her *poisson en papillote* was beyond compare, she won't pick up a knife anymore. The diners could never possibly find, in the eating, what she found in the making.

THE SEVENTH THIRTEENTH

Learnèd Helplessness

Tip of the Icepick

*I hate, more than my accusers, those
who make me accuse myself.*

Bellatrix Sakakino headed an archaeological expedition in the New Mexico desert. They found a spot likely to produce ancient bones and started digging.

Nearly at once, a tremendous dinosaur bone was unearthed—a prodigious find. Everyone was thrilled.

Soon after, they found a bone from a second dinosaur, as momentous a discovery as the first. And right away, another bone. Then one more.

Bone after bone came out of the pit. Large bones and small, ancient but in excellent condition, in a variety never before seen. So many appeared, at such a rate, that the researchers gave up trying to classify them and simply heaped them next to the pit. This went on for days.

One morning, Bellatrix, gazing first upon the pile of bones, then upon the pit, made a queer discovery: there were clearly too many bones to have come out of a pit of that size.

She was certain that, even if the team tried putting all the bones back again (which would be absurd, considering the level of research funding invested in this expedition), they would never fit. The expedition had found too much data about the past to have been contained in the slice of the past they'd dug into. Too much *past*, not enough *pit*.

"Now," wondered Bellatrix, "how do you account for that?"

Verbigeration

The last two customers in the pharmacy: an elderly couple who appear to be arguing in sign language.

Bellatrix Sakakino sat down to write me a love letter. It took her hours, but she only managed to write a single sentence. She read it over and thought, "It's too long."

She cut a few words here and there. She made sure to cut only the most meaningful words. (That's Bellatrix for you.) But for some reason, the sentence got longer.

The more meaningful words she cut, the longer the sentence got.

The more erasers she wore out, the more sheets of paper she found she needed.

In the end, her one-sentence love letter was miles and miles and miles long—and had no words in it.

Virus sin nombre

Tonight, again, you've fooled time into passing.

Poor Elaine Gruber. One might put her life story into a single paragraph. She designed climate control systems for aircraft, lived in a modest condominium, cooked her own meals, and swam to keep fit. In early adulthood, she developed a singular disorder. When she spoke, at unpredictable intervals she snorted. The snort was produced by an involuntary inhalation through both mouth and nose mid-sentence, often mid-word, sounding something like the word "hick". As one might imagine, this unfortunate personal habit was discomfiting to listeners. But what made it truly noteworthy was the fact that Ms. Gruber was perfectly unaware of it. Not only was she unable to perceive her own snorting, but, whenever someone was both kindly disposed and forward enough to mention it, she could not understand them. Their words would, to all outward appearance, pass her by unmarked; her only reaction might be a defocusing of the gaze, from which she emerged after the briefest interval. Unsurprisingly, she was not a popular woman. New acquaintances gave her polite leeway at first, suspended judgment as long as they were able, and eventually avoided her; co-workers made semi-tacit jests not intended to elicit laughter; waiters, cashiers, and civil servants frowned and dealt with her promptly, then found other things to busy themselves with. She had a few permanent friends, none impressive characters themselves, and for this she quite unfairly scorned them. Elaine Gruber was aware of her ill fit with the world but never ascertained its cause. She didn't finish as a suicide, nothing so dramatic, but wended toward the end of life perplexed and disengaged. She was not a dull-witted woman: plenty intelligent enough to realize that things were not with her as they were with others, but never understanding why.

Native Adjectising

*A friendly country with friendly folk—
to feel welcome here, never learn the language.*

Bellatrix Sakakino's parents raised her as the subject of a peculiar experiment. Let me tell you how it worked.

From birth to age five, they kept her strictly isolated from human society, only allowing contact they could mediate. At all times, her parents and any visitors wore specially designed helmets. Each looked like a motorcycle helmet with the visor down, with small external speakers mounted by each cheek and a microphone installed within. The helmets were linked by radio so that wearers could communicate.

The purpose of these helmets was, via an onboard modulator, to convert the wearer's speech to a digital squeal, essentially the noise of an old dial-up modem. What came out of the external speakers was this squealing. This was all Bellatrix was permitted to hear by way of speech for the duration of the experiment.

Bellatrix grew up immersed exclusively in communication of this form. Language as modem shrieks.

The astonishing result was that she did indeed learn to discern meaning from the electronic squeals. When bid to clean up her toys or change into her pajamas, she obeyed. She laughed at silly jokes, grew teary when scolded. Her parents had built a demodulator into the helmet as well, so that, if Bellatrix were to learn to produce modem speech, it might be transformed into human speech within the earpieces. But this functionality never saw use. Her vocal cords were incapable of generating such noises, try as she might; she could understand her parents but never answer them in kind.

Shortly after Bellatrix turned five years old, her parents split up, their years of couples counseling having gone nowhere. Neither was in a position to tend her during this period, so the experiment was halted, and she was sent to live with her maternal grandmother. It was at Grandma Sumako's that she finally learned human speech.

All this was decades ago. Bellatrix is grown now. Over the years, she lost the ability to understand modem noise. So she is, presumably, just like you and me.

But her deepest and most cherished memories are of bedtime stories and lullabies communicated in a tender, loving electronic screech. Princesses who tzzed, ambling through enchanted forests that skreed and skrawed. Stars twinkling like diamonds in the sky, skrrking and brrzing Bellatrix to innocent rest. Expressions of parental love, all in a language she has lost.

She'd give anything to get it back.

Creeping Infallibility

Before you behave in rational self-interest,
you must decide in whose interest you will behave.

In simpler times, the mind was a lone decision-maker, a homunculus in a central control room surrounded by levers and panels.

But today's world is complicated. No one person can run things alone. The modern mind is, more than anything, a bureaucracy.

A decision is needed. One office originates a proposal. The review process begins.

Every time the proposal crosses another desk, it's modified. One department is responsible for thinking about the future. Another promotes present and immediate desires. There's a morality division, a sexual urges division, a greed and acquisitiveness (G&A) division. There's an office (perpetually underfunded) of logic and general principles. In the executive suite on the top floor are the chambers of the minister of pride. Each of them adds, deletes, or amends passages in the draft.

Office politics! Shucks!

Finally, a decision. And, like with the published announcements of a bureaucracy, nobody is sure whose idea it was, nobody is responsible for it, and nobody is entirely happy with the result.

Squelette articulé

The machine says "Thank you" so I don't have to.

The chances of success for any project can be greatly increased by running a simulation beforehand. Common problems can be avoided, and innovative solutions can be discovered. It's just a common-sense best practice.

That's why, before Bellatrix Sakakino was born, an institute in Tokyo decided to simulate her. At first, the two-person research team looked into software-based simulation solutions. But there were so many variables, and so many proprietary licensing fees, that, in the end, they decided a virtual model wasn't achievable within the budget.

They went with a wetware simulation instead. They were able to fabricate the building blocks of the model in a quick ten-minute window and with no significant usage of resources or special facilities. The senior researcher (the one with naming rights for the project) was particularly pleased by the outcome of this implementation.

Forty weeks later, after a procedure that was physically challenging to the junior researcher (the one lacking naming rights; this researcher's name has thus been lost to the records), the Bellatrix wetware model was online.

The advantage of wetware simulation is that it produces highly accurate data. The Bellatrix simulation behaves indistinguishably from a real-world Bellatrix. Because it consumes precisely the same resources and provides exactly the same output, it is highly predictive of how an actual Bellatrix would function.

There are no benefits without costs, of course. The main downside of this technique is the time it requires. The simulation runtime is essentially as long as one wetware lifetime—estimated, as of 2021, at 84.79 years. This is a limitation that cannot be ignored when considering this kind of solution.

Nevertheless, the team is now closely observing her, eager to see the Bellatresque behavior she will predict.

A Purloined Hitherside

That you caught me red-handed is also your fault.

Laurence Sakakino is taking up the entire living room sofa, squashing jellybeans in a smartphone game, when he notices his older sister thrusting out her lower jaw and going crosseyed trying to look down at it. He says, "Um."

"If you think about it," says Bellatrix, face purpling with effort, "people in ancient times never could've seen their own teeth."

"Mirrors." Laurence reapplies himself to his jellybeans.

"Before they invented mirrors. They'd just assume their teeth looked like what everybody else's looked like."

Laurence shuts his eyes. Exhales. Massages bridge of nose with forefinger and thumb. Reflections in water, he doesn't say. Or knocked-out teeth. Or even just horse sense and more important ancient-people problems to deal with.

"The first mirror would have been revolutionary," continues Bellatrix. "Before that, there were so many parts of your body that you'd never get to see. The small of your back. Or," she points at the base of her throat, "this little dent between your collarbones."

"Even the perineum," Laurence intones in science-guy voice. She won't know the word.

"Right." She hasn't got time for whatever joke he's cracking. "If you think about it, there's things *nobody* could see. Like the *inside* of your teeth. I mean, the backsides of your front teeth. But you just angle a mirror in there, and boom, centuries of ignorance wiped away."

"Epochal." Laurence unsofas himself with a huffy grunt and wanders off.

Bellatrix barely notes his departure. Since early childhood, she has been peripherally aware of the tiny bumps and odd ridges on the inner side of her upper incisors. Never before has it occurred to her to wonder about them.

In the hall bathroom, she stands before Laurence's pantograph-mounted shaving mirror and angles her compact mirror around in her mouth. It isn't easy; she keeps tilting it right when she means left, left when she means right. Finally, she sees.

Are those—letters?

They can't be. But they are. On the inner face of each upper incisor is etched, in shallow bas-relief, a tiny ideograph.

"Holy shit," mutters Bellatrix. "Oh, my God."

The four symbols are not kanji, which she knows how to read; nor do they appear to be hangul or simplified Chinese. They looked like no language she's heard of.

How? she marvels. How did they get there? How could I be nineteen years old and only now realize that... that I've got... and... and, seriously, how in the living fuck?

Each ideograph is shaped as if to fit within a square. Their lines are sinuous, their corners angular. They could be from some ancient language lost to history. Or from beyond planet Earth. They're—what are they?

And what are they doing scrimshawed into her teeth?

How long has she—? Well, since forever, when she considers it. All these years. Who put them there? Was she born with—no, impossible.

Is she the only one?

And—what about her dentist?

She has had, what, four different dentists since childhood? Surely they'd have seen these symbols. None ever said a thing.

My God, she thinks, not noticing she has dropped her compact in the sink.

THE EIGHTH THIRTEENTH

The Heckler's Veto

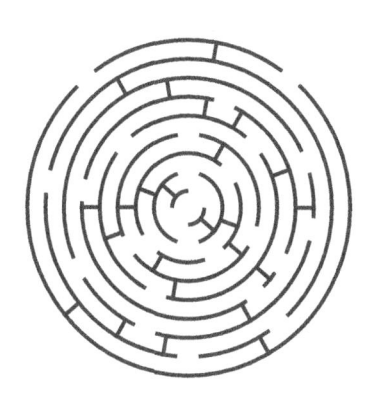

Pontengisme

Lust, malcontentment—you build yourself
a mousetrap: the bait is the mouse.

Droves of ξ mill about on this side of the barbed wire-topped fence. On the other side are wide open fields of dusky flesh. Temptation drives everyone mad. Howling like macaques. Tumbling over one another in unquenchable lust. Grasping through rents in the chain link.

It's pandæmonium. Bellatrix Sakakino cannot watch. An expression of sadness traverses her cheek.

Though she had been sure she was like a penitent on the northern wastes, waiting perseveringly for the grand and the sweeping, she now finds that even she is just another ξ lusting for dusky flesh.

She hyperventilates. Claws at her clothing.

Oh, such guilt.

∽

But then the night sky yawns like a lion, and it starts to rain nails. Bellatrix raises her slender arms, wrapped in barbed wire, and tries to shield herself.

Bacteria that gobble oxygen swarm around her. She panics. Can't breathe.

Several thousand decadent and dissipated businesspersons wearing unnecessary hats all loosen their neckties, cling to the barbed wire-wrapped handrails of the swaying trains, and grow nauseous. Bellatrix sees this and also grows nauseous.

Then emptiness arrives. A shallow, bloodclabbered, alkaline, bonfire-huffing, mundane emptiness that shreds philosophy and sprinkles it on the face of the waters. Her body is wedged between its teeth.

Fetters sprout from her ankles. She shakes them off, and they sprout again. Grief flakes like rust from the chains.

She finally falls into the corner of a trompe-l'œil and tries to conceal herself till dawn.

∼

Dawn breaks and Bellatrix rises. She has not walked far when she runs up against a gang of tough young philosophers. Wearing leather togas. One toying with Occam's switchblade. "You're on *our* turf," scowls the leader. "Let's get *ad hominem* on this bitch!"

She sprints up a darkened alleyway, scrambles over another chain link fence. They hoot and catcall behind her, but she has gotten away.

A city square. Public sculptures, stone benches—and a great crowd of ξ. Droves of ξ, walking but unconscious. They look like slim warm aliens.

There's a skeleton in my skin, she muses, moved by the sight. *I'm always too early for early. I'm always running late for late.* She swoons.

A ξ stumbles dreamily past, thrice-three-times as lovely as necessary. "You just want my tongue on your injuries, don't you?" she croons in the ξ's uncomprehending ear.

But a wave of heat knocks her down. Glass-blowers sweat rivers as the fire burns high. Sea and sky are contending for mastery. "We've got your number now," they say. She cannot stand against the gale.

She sees a ξ walking through the storm, but he is not blown by it. He is sealed in an administrative vacuüm. He is the nosy man of everyplace.

The Heckler's Veto | 93

Bellatrix knows him of old, and says to him, "I'm never too surprised by the cloudy way you glide by—the replies you try not to supply—the elided love you yet deny."

And the nosy man of everyplace retorts, "Your up-and-at-'em attitude has fully wrecked my rotten mood. I find it tedious to say why I can't stand the easy way you still continue to survive but never really feel alive."

This is Bellatrix's mournful rejoinder: "Nothing but a dissipated sinner out to hustle up another dinner—your low unquiet soul and vain ambitions; never hungry but for what you're missing."

And, this longtime dudgeon finally shed, she rests her head on the chopping block and awaits his swashing blow.

∽

All the while, as Bellatrix sleeps, her guardian angel hovers over her.

"I wish I could protect you," he whispers, "on those rare occasions when people take your side—and you deserve for them to.

"You built your castle of ten-yen coins. I wish I could dim your vision." He sighs. "Fate could give you relief – but perhaps I can't.

"I wish all these blinding lights would stop flashing at you," he murmurs fondly. "I wish you could stop losing your shit."

The guardian angel gazes wistfully on her frail fingers resting on the coverlet. "Good people will always hate you," he thinks sadly. "Only the guardian angel community even really sees you. Oh, how we ache."

But deep inside the contrevoyant dream, Bellatrix thinks, "I am *not* a problem to be solved. I am *not* sadness seeking happiness."

She frowns in her sleep. "I'm nature's mistake."

If she could meet her guardian angel, she'd cashier his mawkish ass. The reason? She'll never *understand* him, and he'll never *understand* her.

You've Got Ruin Value

*Underlit office space: less chance of being
caught crying at your desk.*

You're a chimney sweep, stuck in a narrow London chimney. Choking on soot. Cinders in your eyelashes.

Your mates pull your arms from above, but no luck. They pull your legs from below, but you won't budge.

So they bring in lubricating smoke. The smoke builds up from below, piles and piles of it, billowing. It seeps between your skin and the sharp grit of the bricks.

When the smoke has moistened you up, they give you another good tug on the trouser legs, and out you slide.

They carry you into a tavern, lay you on a great oaken table, and ply your throat with ale. It's like sand going down. Everyone laughs at how red your face turns.

After much coughing and hacking, you're finally able to sit up and speak. "Feeling much better, lads."

So, another bracing drink for your ordeals. Three cheers, a slap on the back, and they send you back to work.

Spillikins

A necessary evil is still evil. You're still going to hell.

When otherwise healthy people began dying of heart failure in great numbers, it took scientists and authorities a while to realize what was going on. The dead appeared on all continents, from all walks of life. Only after some months was the crisis even recognized as such; but when the data were collected and analyzed, it was found that sixty to one hundred persons per minute were inexplicably breathing their last.

When leading scientists discovered that the cause was Bellatrix Sakakino's heartbeat, reactions varied from incredulous to horrified. (Never mind how they determined this—it was highly technical.) Every time her heart pulsed, another stopped.

Her heartbeat had already claimed, by one estimate, more than ten million random people in three months. To leave her alive was unacceptable; even knocked unconscious, she would kill vast numbers. World leaders took swift action. A team of assassins was dispatched to bring her down.

The three-pronged assassination attempt failed when the sniper, the man holding the detonation switch, and the poisoner all fell down dead within seconds of each other. Rotten luck!

A second team was mobilized.

As for Bellatrix? She had no inkling until she heard the news, as you and I did, from television. "But—I'm not *trying* to kill anybody!" she cried.

There were pleas in the media not to panic her. The physical exertion of fleeing, or even the stress of awaiting execution, were certain to raise her heart rate, and thus the death toll. But panic she did. She ran, hid, trembled, bemoaned her fate. Contemplated suicide for humanitarian reasons. Couldn't do it.

The snipers found her at last. "Terminate on sight," came the order. Just in the time the man took to level and steady his rifle, her heart, beating on, claimed more lives.

"It's not my *fault* that—" Bellatrix was thinking the instant a bullet cored her skull like an apple.

You and I saw it live on the news.

"Oh, my God," you said, turning to me with eyes full of pity. "It wasn't her *fault* that—I mean, what if it had been you or me instead?"

I hummed and nodded, deciding to keep mum. Shit happens. I was simply glad I still had a pulse.

Lives Forgone in Worlds Fantastical

When again you descend the mountain,
never forget how lovely the lowland looked.

The idea of a catastrophe—a crippling disease; the death of her husband Timothy or of her adult daughter Louisa; or, less cruel and more wonderful, total economic ruin—sometimes captivates her imagination as she's at her desk. Slides, spreadsheets, purchase orders.

In her head she compiles lists of things she'll never know: realms of physics, chemistry, the biological sciences—technical obscurities, the way you put together a circuit or a microchip—the languages of the world, ancient customs, the personal life of the Pope, secret knowledge—is there actually a conspiracy at the top? do all the things that cause cancer, *really* cause cancer? what will people do with their lives in a thousand years?—the religions that will spring up; the way to throw a vase on the wheel; her abortion in high school and what could have happened instead; her father never smiling till he'd drunk two fingers of gin after dinner... She'd like some answers.

Things aren't bad, at home or at work; she has no complaints. But.

You Put the Speck in Speculation

Peek behind each trembling leaf.

Bellatrix Sakakino is among the isotope smokers, at their invitation. She feels honored—overawed.

Languid, beautiful people with flawless posture. Poetic necklines. Admirable decadence. They hate Bellatrix, and quite reasonably, for she isn't as good as them.

"This beauty you see in us," they complain, "is false. We wear this earthly garment only till it spoils, like fruit fallen to earth."

"Oh, what can *you* know?" they scoff. "What have *you* felt of the burdens of mortality? Thy life, lost, were not lost at all. Knowest thou the tenth part of the anguish of the lovely?" One calls her *häßlich*. The others nod and smoke, earnestly.

"The body," declaims one, "is a box of water." The others nod and smoke again.

"There is a lyricism," offers another, "in the leaching away of youthful charm." He is a maverick; the others regularly ignore him; but this time his invocation of lyricism has struck a chord. All nod and smoke.

Bellatrix dares to interject: "Were I religious, I would pray: *God rob me of all I love; tear every joy from me; cast me into incalculable misery, so that my suffering doth wax beyond mortal endurance—for then shall I begin to deserve what I have lost.*"

Then she waits for a response. Any kind of reaction. One of the smokers kicks her from behind. She falls over.

With her face on the ground, hemmed by enemies, Bellatrix forgets all. She gazes down into the dirt. She digs up a bit of earth with her fingers. Under it, she sees frost needles. *Frost needles.* Perfectly formed. If she hadn't looked at them, it's likely no one ever would have.

Nyetovshchik

To every question, I answer, "No."
Why? Because I hate to be wrong.

As I imagine you know, there's a protocol for getting into an elevator.

The first to board occupies one corner. Probably a front corner—that's where the buttons are.

The second takes the other front corner.

The third will take one of the rear corners. Which they take isn't prescribed, but often, to distance themself as much as possible from the second rider, they will take the corner behind the first.

The fourth takes the only remaining unoccupied corner. Viewed from above, the riders' positions resemble the dots on the "4" face of a die.

A fifth rider will have no choice but to stand in the middle, becoming the center dot on the "5" face of the die. If even more people board, the clean symmetry is wrecked and the elevator becomes merely crowded.

No one ever sat me down and said, "Look, son, here's how you board an elevator." Yet I do it too. Do you? It wouldn't surprise me if you did.

I suppose it's natural you'd not want to stand near me, nor I near you.

Antapocatastatic Peace

All his life, he was one man away from catastrophe.

On Monday, you lost your depth perception. The world became a screen.

On Tuesday, you became unable to apprehend the passage of time. Cause and effect came unglued. Memory was a filing cabinet with its papers spilled onto the floor.

On Wednesday, you lost the sense of sight. Toes were stubbed.

On Thursday, you were deprived of the senses of smell and taste in tandem. Milk and whisky, cabbage and beefsteak, biscuits and prunes were all reduced to differing textures.

On Friday morning, the left ear went. You walked in circles for an hour before realizing. The right ear lasted till mid-afternoon.

On Saturday, your limbs ballooned like sausages. You curled into a fetal ball, wept for a time, and, ready at last to slip into a contrevoyant dream, slipped out of this one.

THE NINTH THIRTEENTH
Bureaucracide

My Memoirs Won't Mention Me

You're a draft. Circulating past everyone.

Have you seen my latest action movie? Below are some key scenes.

- Scene 3: The Soulless Lunatic murders the Reluctant Bruiser's girlfriend.
- Scene 4: The Reluctant Bruiser vows revenge. This wrong must be righted. The Soulless Lunatic shall pay.
- Scene 19: The Reluctant Bruiser is in the Atmospheric Old Building, getting important information from the Shifty Informant. The Soulless Lunatic creeps up the stairs, aiming to kill them both. A Security Guard jumps out: "Hey, you can't come up h—" Bang! The Soulless Lunatic shoots him dead, then keeps climbing the stairs without missing a beat. This shows how soulless the Lunatic is.
- Scene 26: The Security Guard, whose name is revealed to have been Greg Collins, is mourned by his disconsolate widow.
- Scene 27: Greg Collins's children will grow up missing their father terribly.
- Scene 28: Greg Collins's mother's heart breaks at the death of her son. He was her last surviving child.

Scene 29: Down at the bar, Greg Collins's friends hold an impromptu wake. He will never be forgotten.

Scene 40: A news montage shows that the Soulless Lunatic is still at large, and that the Reluctant Bruiser—wrongfully framed—is also wanted by the police. This ratchets up the tension a notch.

Scene 40-a: The news anchor reminds viewers of the death of Greg Collins, beloved husband, father, and son, killed by the Soulless Lunatic in Scene 19.

Scene 68: After the Breathtakingly Destructive Car Chase, the Reluctant Bruiser corners the Soulless Lunatic in an abandoned factory. As the music rises to a triumphant pitch, he aims his gun at the Soulless Lunatic and grimly says, "This is for my girl—"

Scene 68-a: "—and Greg Collins—"

Scene 68-b: "—you evil bastard!" Bang! The Reluctant Bruiser shoots the Soulless Lunatic dead. All wrongs have been righted. The Soulless Lunatic has paid.

(Note: As you may have realized if you've seen the movie, scenes 26 through 29, 40-a, and 68-a were removed by the studio in post-production. That's just the sort of crap you have to put up with in the motion picture business.)

Antediluvian Optimism

Redundant systems and safety features, gradually eliminated.
(Nothing has gone wrong so far.)

"Before we begin," Bellatrix, traveler of many worlds, says to you, "I had better explain how trees reproduce."

She directs your attention to a sketch of an apple tree on the chalkboard. "Certain trees have evolved to reproduce by enveloping their seeds in tasty fruit. An animal scarfs the fruit, moseys up the road, takes a dump—and the seed lands in a pile of fresh manure."

"Ideal conditions," you observe, "to grow a new tree."

"Precisely." Bellatrix sweeps a hand toward her many-worlds viewer. "Come."

It is a queer-looking contraption, all vacuum tubes, rivets, and brass dials. Bellatrix diddles and twiddles the controls. With a theremin-like squawk, a shaky image swims into view on the cathode-ray screen.

"Behold."

You peer at it. A human female in primitive attire creeps along a forest trail no more swiftly than a loris. From the bushes leaps a fearsome tiger, and—oh, God! It rips into her, devouring her frightfully fast. You can barely watch.

The image wavers, and the tiger is in a different part of the forest. It squats onto its haunches for a moment, then, circling the spot, kicks dirt over it before wandering off.

The image again wavers. From the ill-concealed tiger dung, something comes wriggling out: a human child, barely able to crawl. Another emerges, and another. Each moves painfully slowly, and you begin to fear for them. What if there's another tiger around?

The picture goes black. You turn to see Bellatrix, her finger on a switch. "Enough. You understand?"

"Not quite."

Bellatrix, many-worlds traveler, smiles triumphantly. "In that world," she explains, "human reproduction works like those trees I have mentioned. A human must be eaten and pooped out by a tiger. Only thus can new humans be born. Now, a question: In such a world, what sort of humans will naturally evolve?"

You wait to allow her to answer her own question.

"Slow-moving humans who taste good to tigers." She nods and folds her arms.

Something about this just feels... *wrong* to you. Being a slow-moving human who tastes good to tigers seems a *terrible* state of affairs. "Why would evolution deal them such a losing hand?"

Bellatrix smiles condescendingly. "Don't worry," she purrs. "In our own world, that's not how things work at all."

Faute de mieux

Our investigation finds it suspicious that we investigated you.

Our farm was suffering. The rains poured down in autumn, and floods rushed across the meadows and carried off the topsoil. Nothing would grow.

To firm up the soil, you got the idea to introduce four-leafed owl grass. The grass roots would interlock and hold the soil together. And it worked.

But the four-leafed owl grass grew out of control and began to choke off the crops. So I got the idea to introduce African rock weevils. The rock weevils would chew up the roots of the owl grass and kill it off. And it worked.

But the black bullfrogs that feed on rock weevils bred like wildfire. And black bullfrog dung is copper-rich and gets into the water, and then the oxen get diarrhœa and won't breed. So you got the idea to introduce diamondback pythons to eat the bullfrogs. And it worked.

But diamondback python mating calls are shrill, and they spook the chickens so that they stop laying eggs. So I got the idea to introduce cotton-foxes to eat the python eggs. And it worked.

But cotton-foxes also eat the waterbugs that usually clear the ponds of algae. The algae flourished and blocked up the sluices. The topsoil, lacking moisture, dried out and loosened, and the next time the autumn rains came, the topsoil was washed away.

So you suggested, "Four-leafed owl grass?"
And I replied, "What other choice do we have?"

Geomancing the Stone

Just as our enemies might, if they knew us as our friends do, love us more, so might our friends, if they knew us as strangers do, hate us less.

So, building a computer more massive than the universe—I suppose you wonder why I took the trouble. Not to mention whether it was worth it. Of course it was!

Look, you may think you're a rational and free being. You may think you're a smoky, romantic mystery. Ha!

In fact, all matter in the universe, down to the very molecules and atoms, obeys predictable laws. Since even the human mind—really nothing more than a shadow cast by the chemical coruscations of the brain—also behaves according to fixed laws, all that you do is predetermined by biology, chemistry, and ultimately the immutable momentum of the chain of events initiated by the Big Bang; and thus your freedom is a *silly illusion*.

Having determined the laws which govern matter, all I had to do was build an enormous computer.

And all I had to input into this computer was the precise location and status of every molecule in the universe at a given instant.

Thereupon, all the computer had to do was apply the algorithm that describes the behavior of matter, and it calculated for me exactly what would happen in the future of the universe, as far forward as I might care to know.

And given this knowledge, it was child's play—child's play!—to determine whether you would choose the arrabbiata or the bolognese at supper, whether you would put on brown socks or gray the next morning, and whether you would slap Denise in the face or sink into silent mortification when she confessed her extramarital affairs.

We come now to the aforementioned complication (picayune, really): data describing the precise location and status of a molecule requires more than one molecule's worth of storage space, so my computer, to hold such data for every molecule in the universe, had to be more massive than the universe.

Assembling enough matter to build the sucker was, I admit, arduous.

But I did it! And as a result, I've figured you out.

Faitiche

If the shoe fits, blame the shoe.

"Why has my litmus paper turned blue?" I demand of the professor. I'm positively fit to be tied.

She equably explains, "Because you put an alkaline on it."

"*That's* the reason?"

"Yes."

"But... but... is it a *good* reason?"

Such a basic question, and she can't answer it. Why'd they make her a professor, then?

I clear out of the lab and head home. There, I find that a hurricane has come and blown down my house. I cry out, "Why is my house reduced to sticks and timbers?"

The neighbors patiently answer, "Because a hurricane blew it down."

But I retort, "No, *why*? Whose fault is it? Whose responsibility? Who can I blame?"

"It's the hurricane's fault," the neighbors tell me. "The hurricane is responsible. Blame the hurricane."

Which actually checks out, if you think about it.

Cancellist

The wounds time heals fastest are those of the wounder.

Bellatrix Sakakino was pretty deep in debt. After falling further and further behind on her loan payments, she resigned herself to the fact: she just wasn't ever going to be able to pay it back.

So she went down to the bank, walked into the bank manager's office, and punched him in the cheek.

She grabbed documents from his desk and ripped them up.

She peed on his swivel chair.

She called him a liar, communist, child pornographer, and deadbeat dad—right to his face.

She chewed on his necktie like a dog worrying a squirrel.

And then she collapsed in tears, hid her face in shame, and said, choking back sobs, "I know—I know you can never forgive me. I can never atone for this. I'm sure you never want to see me again."

Off she ran. And you know how the story ends: the bank, so glad to be rid of her, never forced her to make good on her obligations. A neat trick!

Á sjálf sig þau trûðu

*"You can't be stepped in by the same
person twice," said the river.*

Bellatrix Sakakino was not exactly a liar—rather, she tinted the truth in hues of self-interest. Nor was she, in her own judgment, conniving or manipulative. It was no crime to want what was best for herself, and to lean on folks to sway them her way. You could wait all winter for the wind to blow a tree down, or you could give it a notch with the ax.

Her siblings, Marlon and Heidi, were unsurprised to learn that Bellatrix had convinced their mother to alter her Will. Most of the money was to go to big sister Bella. Marlon and Heidi could easily imagine, though not prove, the guilt-mongering, wheedling, unfair constructions of past events, selective recounting of conversations, and other tactics Bellatrix must have used. Naturally, they were bitter about it.

But when their mother passed away—carried off by an embolism no one in the family had looked for, all assuming her recurrent cancer would claim her—it shocked Bellatrix severely. Her mother's was a death that Bellatrix had long anticipated but never properly believed in; certain events, at certain times, can jog the most calcified of hearts. Bellatrix looked within herself, and into her past acts, and found little to like.

When the probate judge outlined how the Will divided the inheritance, awarding nearly all to Bellatrix, Marlon could not contain himself. "Is that really even *fair*?"

"Why wouldn't it be?" asked the judge; so Marlon described how he had always known Bellatrix to be: crafty, egoistic, and pushy.

Though nothing Marlon said could alter the Will, Bellatrix felt goaded to self-defense. "I've changed," she claimed. She told the judge and her siblings how, in recent days, immersed in self-reflection, she had discovered shame at her past behavior and had resolved to fundamentally alter who she was. Where once she had been craven, now she would be frank; where once sly, now forthright; where once self-absorbed, now meek and fair to all. As they listened, the others gradually found themselves impressed by the open honesty and emotional conviction of her address.

"I can truly say," she concluded, "that the old Bellatrix Sakakino no longer exists."

The probate judge cleared her throat. "A person who does not exist cannot inherit property." She found that the entire inheritance should be divided between Marlon and Heidi.

"But—is that really even *fair*?" cried Bellatrix.

THE TENTH THIRTEENTH

Your Ruined Septum

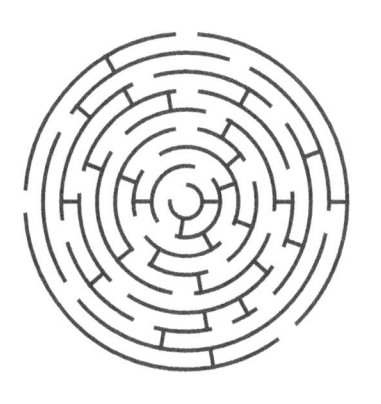

Manywhere

If the crescent moon at the start of the month is an opening parenthesis, and the crescent moon at the end of the month is a closing parenthesis, then all the month but the night of the new moon is merely an aside.

Bellatrix Sakakino received a mysterious package in the post: a thumb drive folded within a sheet of A4 paper which read, in black Sharpie, "I thought you should know."

On the drive were innumerable massive files she had no clue how to open, but she didn't need to. In the top directory was a text document named Read Me First. What it said left her thunderstruck.

She learned that, immediately after she was born, the obstetrician had harvested blood rich in stem cells from her umbilical cord, and researchers had used a revolutionary laboratory technique to make an exact clone of her, with one difference. By altering the DMRT1 gene on the ninth chromosome, they had made the clone male. She and her unknown twin were otherwise genetically identical. Only their sexes were reversed.

According to the thumb drive, his name was Nao Hovgaard. He worked in a hair salon in Hamadayama, just up the Inokashira Line. She made an appointment for a trim.

Not fifteen minutes after she settled into the swivel chair and he draped a vinyl cover over her, with surreal ease they fell in love. There was no other word for it but fate. To keep things simple, she pretended it had been a chance meeting. They saw each other daily after that.

He was ten months her junior, but neither cared. The tendency to muse during lulls in conversation—the dislike of crowds or loud public spaces—the almost pathological antipathy toward uninteresting tasks... Their similarities were striking. One morning, Nao commented dreamily on this. "It's like I was designed to be with you. Like, on the genetic level."

Bellatrix, uneasy, murmured, "Genetics don't determine everything, though."

"You're wrong." His hair had fallen over his face, covering one eye. "People only think they're free." He looked so alluring, half obscured.

"But that's..." Lost again in him, she never completed the thought.

She should have thrown out the thumb drive, or at least hidden it better. He'd been watching YouTube when she drifted to sleep one Sunday after lunch; when she awoke, his face was drained white.

"How much did you read?"

"Everything."

"I was going to tell you," she lied.

He stared, rigid. "Our kids would be... inbred." Nao had always wanted children.

Bellatrix began silently to cry. "Self-bred." *They would be us*, she wanted to add, to protest. *Wholly one hundred percent us. Parents love children who are half them, so we would love our children twice as much. Wholly.*

"God, how... creepy." He shut the door gently when he left.

As I love you wholly. It was no use. She could never have won him back because she could never have reconciled two things she knew at her core: That he was right, and that he was wrong. She was wiser than he, and she was a fool.

Your Ruined Septum | 119

Years passed, but the pain of love never faded. All her life till the moment they'd met had been a prelude, she often reflected; her every day since, a lingering note. She walked as one dead, hollowed out by loneliness, and she never forgave him for thwarting her fate.

Nam deteriores omnes sumus licentiæ

"Please, doctor, cure my self-hatred—but not yet."
—*Augustine, to his psychiatrist*

"You're evil," I said.
"Ad hominem," said the Devil. "Fallacious."
"God will punish you," I said.
"Ab auctoritate," said the Devil. "Fallacious."
"Everyone knows you're bad," I said.
"Ad populum," said the Devil. "Fallacious."
"You're distorting the argument because you're evil," I said.
"Petitio principii," said the Devil. "Fallacious."
"So, prove me wrong, then," I said.
"Onus probandi," said the Devil. "Fallacious."
"Until you appeared, humans were virtuous," I said.
"Post hoc ergo propter hoc," said the Devil. "Fallacious."
"Evil could only come from you," I said.
"E silentio," said the Devil. "Fallacious."
"But you're evil!" I cried.
"Ad nauseam," said the Devil. "You lose."
Dang it.

Stepping Gingerly

"Break," pray young women to their hearts.

It was a freak accident: not only was Bellatrix Sakakino's left leg sheared clean off just above the knee, but also a shard of shrapnel was embedded in her medula hypocallosum—the part of her brain that should have retained the knowledge that she'd lost her leg.

For the rest of her life, she fell down again and again. And again, and again.

Desengaños del mundo

*To mistake facts for feelings, feelings
for facts: one kind of suffering.*

You were shipwrecked and adrift on the high sea, and the other castaways decided to kill and eat you. But not every part of you.

Some bits, they ate. Other bits, they tossed over the side of the lifeboat. Boy, were you mad!

But honestly? Don't flatter yourself. Not every bit of you was tasty.

maltnalt your grlp

*"This product does not generate
dioxin when burnt," said the dioxin.*

Bellatrix Sakakino began to worry about her weight. "My belly's starting to stick out," she thought. "Maybe I'd better diet."

She cut down on how much she ate, especially carbohydrates and sweets. But her stomach continued to grow. And nothing terrified her more than obesity.

So she stopped drinking beer and other alcohol, thinking it would help. But she still got fatter.

She decided to try giving up poker and pachinko, just to see. The same with one-night stands. She got fatter yet.

She donated all her money to charity, and gave everything in her house to anyone who wanted it. But her stomach didn't shrink one millimeter.

Soon she had given up all food, all drink, all sex, all money, all pleasure, all enjoyment, all things.

But she only got fatter, and fatter, and fatter still.

Bumptious Billingsgate

Split-second amusement park drops. What a thrill.

Bellatrix Sakakino was assembling a little set of shelves. She'd found them on clearance, only a thousand yen.

The box they came in looked oddly content. It *was* oddly content. Bellatrix had never realized that cardboard boxes could feel contentment.

The masking tape that sealed the box at the edges and central seam was visibly pleased as well—as though today were a fine day indeed for masking tape. Bellatrix, lacking a proper cutter, sliced into it with her house key. The masking tape looked less pleased after that.

Nevertheless, she drew out the parts. Two side pieces, three shelves, two thin backing pieces only properly varnished on one side, and a plastic baggie with screws.

The two side pieces were clearly feeling chipper today, but the three shelves had an unmistakably aloof air. The two backing pieces cast their gazes about gormlessly. The screws in the baggie were nonplussed, unsure of the situation.

Bellatrix reached for her screwdriver and the instruction sheet that had been enclosed in the cardboard box. The screwdriver was exasperated with her, and the instruction sheet was angry.

"What?" demanded Bellatrix. No answer.

She was used to this treatment from the screwdriver (they had a history), but the fury pulsing from the instruction sheet was a shock. She was further shocked to find, on returning her attention to the shelf pieces, that they had all turned against her as well.

There was no mistaking it. They regarded her with naked *hatred*.

"What?" asked Bellatrix again. She did not sound defiant or demanding now; rather, she sounded bewildered, even hurt. "What did I ever do?"

"Tsk," clucked the pieces. Their tone was not merely annoyed—it was beyond annoyed. "What you *did* isn't the issue." They glowered but would say no more.

Filemot

*Like frightened wood sprites at dawn,
we too must one day scatter.*

Sakakino Unlimited is not a corporation to trifle with. Its reach spans continents, industries, even eras. As a star bends space-time, the mass of its wealth bends life itself.

Sensing a potential for revenue streams in what they call "I.P.", Sakakino has patented adjectives and adverbs. Before anyone may use these classes of words in speech or print, they need to get clearance. And the fees for licensing them? Phew.

You're going to, what? Fight back? File a lawsuit? Tell Bellatrix she can't do that?

Go ahead.

"How depressing," you murmur. "How utterly Sakakinovian." (They hear you, of course. That's three. Your account has been debited.)

Well.

Well, we've got nouns and verbs. That hasn't changed. In a pinch, we can convey the basics of our message.

But do you remember, in your youth, before all this started, the ways we used adjectives and adverbs? Take an adjective like "deep". The night could be deep. Take "mysterious" or "aching". The wind could be mysterious, the dawn aching.

So many years have passed since then.

In your youth, the night *was* deep. The wind *was* mysterious, and the dawn aching.

Things have changed. All those adjectives have been taken from you. Now, night is night. Wind is wind, dawn is dawn.

There are night, wind, and dawn. That's all.

THE ELEVENTH THIRTEENTH

Contrevoyant Dreams

Un poco alterado

*The aged in public, suffering in
public—dispiriting reminders.*

Bellatrix Sakakino worked for a commercial bank, focusing on securities valuation and research, and nobody liked her. This was because of her tints and hues. The colors emanating from her person were too raw and vivid, oversaturated, garish. They struck the eye with nauseating force. She was a crackerjack on the job, but those around her shied away.

One day, she began to fade. She didn't notice at first.

People at the office, finding the sight of her easier to bear, started speaking to her beyond what was necessary. A handful of her coworkers—amiable pastels, chirpy neons, au courant grays—even socialized with her. This was her first clue that she was changing.

As she faded further, she attracted the interest of men. She even, against all expectations, got her first boyfriend: Mark, two years her senior, medium-dark cyan, boyish and graceful. Bellatrix Sakakino, whose soft-focus picture of happiness had always been that of a couple holding hands, finally got a taste of joy.

But still she faded. Others soon had trouble making her out. She'd be in the office pantry or a conference room for several minutes before anyone noticed her. She became translucent; her voice got harder to hear; when she reached for things, she could hardly pick them up. Mark eventually moved on to a more discernible love interest.

It stung, but Bellatrix thought, "Being hard to see is still so much better than being hard to look at." Though she was sad that her observable moment had passed, it was a delicate sugar-crystal sadness, for she had never been as happy as during those weeks when she had faded to just the right softness. "Whatever happens next, I wouldn't have traded that for anything."

And with that, as she stood in the office pantry, Bellatrix's body dissolved into a million transparent particles and was scattered by air currents from the heater vent.

Read 'Em, Wept

A paranoiac sees the world as we all strive to: regimented in a majestic and terrifying design whose sole focus is herself.

Bellatrix Sakakino's feature film directorial debut was a supernatural drama called *All Souls' Day*. It caused a sensation.

Criminal investigators played by Will Smith, Angelina Jolie and Liam Neeson race the clock to save a young girl—and their own souls. In a surprise third-act twist, two of the three principal characters are killed. The other must struggle on alone.

The advance reviews were written and the movie already in theaters before social media began to realize that, depending on where you saw the film, the two characters who died were different.

Posts from Marylanders like, "I literally cried when only Angelina was left standing," were met with retorts from Californians like, "are u retarted?? bitch was the 1st one to b killed smh."

What happened? Did Bellatrix and her crew secretly shoot three different endings? Were three different release prints of the film distributed to theaters without anyone in the industry catching on?

Interviews with the stars revealed that each believed she or he was the only protagonist left at the end of the film.

When pressed on this point, Bellatrix only replied, "They weren't *wrong* about that, now, were they?"

Retroactive Discontinuity

Success—how boring.

Bellatrix Sakakino noticed, abandoned on the luggage rack of her morning commuter train, a bound sheaf of pages. She had to stretch to reach it.

It was a script, like for a play. The title page read, *Bellatrix Sakakino Takes the Train*.

"Holy shit," thought Bellatrix.

She opened to the first page. The stage directions specified that a character called Bellatrix Sakakino comes to the Inokashira Line turnstile. The man in front of her drops his pass and makes the whole line wait. "That really happened today," Bellatrix thought, stunned.

On the station platform in the play, the announcer comes on and informs them of a delay. This had probably also really occurred, though it happened practically every day—she couldn't say for sure.

In the crush as they board the train, a businessman character surreptitiously pinches the Bellatrix character's bum. Sad to say, this had also happened that morning.

On the train, the Bellatrix character notices a bound sheaf of pages on the luggage rack. It's a script, like for a play. The Bellatrix character looks inside it.

"Oh," murmured Bellatrix—the one reading the script, not the one reading the script in the script. "I get it." She felt oddly let down. Nevertheless, she kept reading. The Bellatrix character reads about the dropped train pass, the delay announcement, the sexual harassment. Then, she murmurs, "Oh. I get it." And what she reads next is—

"Shit." Bellatrix slammed shut the script.

There were about a hundred more pages in it. For a moment, she wondered what to do; then, feeling mischievous, she started again from the start.

On donne l'idée du vrai avec du faux

A saint: a failed human.

You raised a statue to Bellatrix Sakakino. This was fitting indeed, considering Sakakino's seminal influence on the New Statuary movement. But it also went without saying that we found the thing intolerable. I organized a protest with the aim of knocking it down. We assembled two blocks away and began marching.

Early in her career, Sakakino endeared herself to us with a monument to Josephine Serre, history's first woman dentist. The statue was lauded for its unearthly grace but drew controversy for what it was made of: tens of thousands of human teeth fused together with epoxy. Some found it poetic; others, repulsive. We in the art world were smitten.

Next came Sakakino's marriage of technology and emotional resonance: her celebration of environmentalist Rachel Carson. Sakakino erected a statue in the Mojave Desert formed of perpetual ice—the symbolism was not subtle—kept frozen from within by an innovative cooling system powered, aptly, by solar energy. It became a site of pilgrimage for climate change activists and a beacon of hope in the face of slow global catastrophe.

Finally, her magnum opus: the Humanity Monument. AI-driven stonecutting robots developed in cooperation with MIT would produce statues of every human being alive. Her algorithms scoured supermassive image banks originally compiled for facial recognition and surveillance software, collecting photographic material of all of humanity. With superhuman speed and precision, the robots extrapolated three-dimensional models from the photos and began carving what promised to be the most democratic and inclusive project of commemoration in history.

Then we learned that Sakakino's lawyers were quietly asserting that, by producing original artwork, she might claim copyright over the likenesses of all living persons. Legal experts differed vociferously on whether this was even possible. It didn't matter; the project collapsed in scandal.

Sakakino's troubles didn't end there. Rumors surfaced that the cooling system of the Carson ice statue was not fully solar-powered. Sakakino's denials were rendered moot when the Earth Liberation Front detonated charges that cut the hidden connection to the San Bernardino County electrical grid and the statue promptly melted.

Six months later, the Washington Post broke the story of a human trafficker in Thailand who had admitted to harvesting thousands of teeth from unwilling donors on behalf of a certain up-and-coming sculptor half a world away. A victims' rights group marched on the Serre statue and tore it down; shaky smartphone footage of the event went viral.

Our group of angry activists looked not unlike those in that iconic video. The same outrage, the same determination. You and I met at the base of the pedestal as my team began throwing grappling hooks. "This statue is a monument to all the beauty she created!" you shouted at me, tears gleaming on your cheeks.

I was having none of it. "What about the lies? The pain and suffering?"

The heavy bronze statue toppled to the street with a tremendous bang. "You're a shitheel!" you screeched, swinging your billy club at my head.

I dodged and, barely missing you with my taser, shouted back, "You're a dumbfuck!" But I regretted this at once. Despite all our quarrels over the years, I knew your heart to be good. Wondering what to say, I recollected a statement Sakakino once made in an interview for The New Statuary Journal shortly after the Carson statue was no more, her tone resigned, even philosophic: *The problem with statues is the same as the problem with people. They deserve to be raised up, yet we are obliged to knock them down.*

I quoted this to you, thinking to score a point in the debate. You knocked me down.

Ignormal

Life is a contest we ought all to have the good sense to lose.

Bellatrix nocks an arrow, steadies the bow, draws back the string, sights the bullseye across the sun-dappled pasture, and, rolling her fingers from the string, looses the arrow. It flashes out in an upward arc and bends swiftly toward the bullseye, certain to hit.

An instant before it reaches its target, the arrow dissipates into multicolored smoke—the head, the shaft, then the feather, all of an instant. The smoke hangs in the breezeless afternoon air, fading.

Bellatrix exhales softly in satisfaction and nocks another arrow.

Tayy al-Arḍ

Common sense:
1) An enemy of reason.
2) A deliverance from the weariness of reason.

Bellatrix Sakakino was out to sea on a luxury cruise ship. Without warning, the engines stopped. "Everyone overboard," came a public address announcement. "We have to push the ship."

The captain, the crew, and all the passengers leapt into the sea. Only Bellatrix stayed aboard, for she hadn't finished her avocado daiquiri. From her vantage, she could see everyone swimming up against the enormous hull to push.

Some worked alone, others in groups. Some pushed mightily, others lackadaisically. Those on opposite sides of the hull sometimes pushed in contrary directions. None could know what the others were doing.

The boat shifted a bit. A little this way, a little that.

A man in the water wearing officer's stripes hollered to Bellatrix. "Hey! Are we making progress?"

She scanned the horizon for any landmark by which to discern their course, but it was ocean in all directions. She glanced upward. There hung the moon, ashen in the afternoon, pulling the whole crushing bulk of the sea imperceptibly toward itself.

"Yes," Bellatrix called down to the officer. "We're moving."

Unring the Bells

The last item on my checklist: "Finish this checklist."

On Bellatrix Sakakino's Last Day, her sister Hannah slept late, woke to the cotton pillowcase cool against her cheek, then ate a slow breakfast: yogurt with honey, homemade raisin bread, cubes of cut melon, black coffee.

Their brother Ambrose sat by the window and read a novel till the sun was well risen, then took a wander outside, sticking to the narrower, quieter streets in Shimokitazawa. There were couples on café patios and hairdressers lounging outside on smoke breaks. The old woman who taught acting classes trundled past on her bicycle. The hookah bar owner hosed down the pavement in front of his corrugated shutters.

When the bell rang just after noon at their grandmother's apartment in Tateishi, Setsu opened the door to find her gentleman friend Okafo bearing Indian curry takeaway and half a dozen record albums. His kindly smile never faltered when Setsu looked blankly at him. "Bella's Last Day," he said, knowing Setsu needed the reminder. "Ah!" laughed Setsu in her usual demure semi-panic, beckoning him inside. "I'll freshen up."

Tatsuya and Abdullah, a couple of Bellatrix's exes, met at the turnstile in Nishi-Ogikubo Station not long before dusk and dapped elaborately as suit-clad commuters shuffled round them. They'd pledged to drain off one *tokkuri* of rice wine at each closet-sized bar in the neighborhood. Each was sure he'd outlast the other.

Hannah and Ambrose chose a dimly lit *anaba* in Nakano for risotto and a chat. They shared a tacit agreement to follow their sister's Last Day rules: no karaoke, no talking about work, no emotional drama; and, as they explained to the bartender, the TV mounted up in the corner needed to be turned off.

Setsu and Okafo strolled from the bus stop back to her place after dinner, arm in arm under the streetlamps, the fingers of her other hand laid over his forearm. Each hummed and laughed lowly, barely able to contain themselves till they got home.

Seven bars into their *hashigo-zake*, Abdullah asked Tatsuya how he was. "I'm going to slow down," Tatsuya mumbled, lowering his cup. Abdullah said, "Yeah, better be careful," then burst into giggles. They spent the next hour on their backs in a narrow neighborhood park, looking at the stars and sharing music from Tatsuya's phone, one earbud each.

With a yawn and a cheek-kiss, Ambrose left earlier than Hannah to clear the way for things with her and the bartender, who was the spitting image of Tomochin from AKB48. Hannah was just tipsy enough to flirt with the girl, just sober enough not to trainwreck.

In all, it wasn't bad for a Last Day. Certainly no funeral could have compared. If Bellatrix could have come back to life for twenty-four more hours, there's no way she'd have wanted to waste that extra day daubing her eyes over somebody's casket. She'd have spent her last day the way they—that handful of people to whom she had mattered—spent it for her.

THE TWELFTH THIRTEENTH

Varied Paralyses

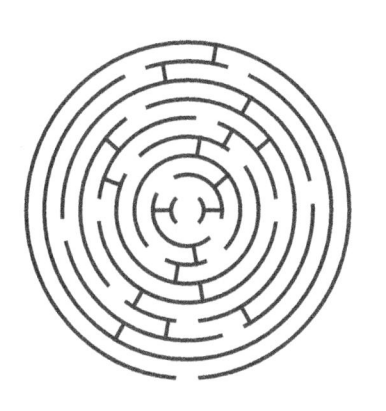

Done and Dusted

He slipped on the road, dropped his box.
All his apples spilled out.
And we laughed at
Clumsiness.

I was with Bellatrix Sakakino on her deathbed. The room was kept dim for her, and warmed by an oil-burning stove. She lay still beneath her quilts, eyes closed. I inquired whether she was comfortable, and she gave a subtle nod.

I imagine she felt the end coming on, for she feebly lifted her hand. I leant in and asked, "What is it?"

"Don't grieve long for me," she murmured. "Rain will fall and settle the dust. When the rainwater dries, it returns to the clouds to rain down again, and the dust, when dry, flies up again. All things must cycle so. We view them for a span, and then we also return to water and dust."

With this, she bowed her head and breathed softly, and I leant back in my chair, very much struck by her serene readiness to meet death.

Perhaps five or so minutes had passed when Bellatrix wrinkled her nose and raised her head slightly, her eyes on me. "You cut one, didn't you?"

I sat nonplussed, then replied, "No, I didn't."

She tutted and rolled her eyes. "You know, I'm only the one *dying* here. I'd rather not go out in a haze of your ass-gas."

"You're imagining it." I really was innocent of the charge.

"Just—go fart in the hall, if you can't hold it in." She dropped her head to the pillow.

A moment later, her eyes opened once more. Over the years, I'd learnt to divine her thoughts from her countenance, and what I read now was rueful annoyance at having ruined the solemn mood established by her prior comments—by what I now saw were to have been her *last words*.

I observed hesitation in her face, and then her mind began to turn. I fancied that I could even trace the course of her thoughts as she prepared to repeat her final words—one last time, once and for all, and then lips sealed till the end. *What was it?* she must have thought. *Don't grieve—dust and rainwater—with the clouds and all that—view them for a spell? Wait, was it for a "spell"? A "spell" sounds too homespun... For the love of Chr—*

Her breath ceased, and her eyes rolled back. Bellatrix was gone.

I suppose I must have wept. She had been dearer to me than I could ever express. But something prevented me from yielding myself entirely to mourning. A trailing dissonance, like a singer hitting a bad note on a song's final syllable.

I do wish Bella could have managed a little longer to keep her mouth shut.

Pass the Freedom Fries

The slick sparkly temptation to be a good person.

Just after I was born, the Devil crept to my side and whispered into my ear: "Choose now what you will be.

"Do you want to be a patient or impatient person?

"Do you want a conservative or a free-wheeling disposition?

"What kind of sense of humor will you give yourself? Bawdy, capricious, self-deprecating?

"Do you choose to be greedy for possessions or detached from them?

"Choose now what sort of food, art, and music you will prefer.

"And choose also whether you will think with your head or your heart."

This is how I answered her: "I cannot choose.

"I've just been born and haven't yet chosen a personality.

"With no personality, I have no preferences or inclinations.

"With no preferences or inclinations, I have nothing influencing me to choose a personality for myself.

"I'm caught in a paradox: being unable to make this first choice, I am incapable of making any. Thus, I have no free will."

The Devil smiled. "I win."

"How so?" I asked.

"If you have no free will," she replied, "then you cannot go to Hell."

Dysregulation

> *I ran into a*
> *Wall. As hard as I*
> *Could. On*
> *Purpose. And broke my*
> *Nose. And I cried*
> *Out, "This wall*
> *Broke my nose."*

No one can see the great malevolent thing like a bird that hovers over Bellatrix, but it is always just above her shoulder, glaring down. As large and stout as a fire hydrant, it has a long curved beak like a scimitar and a heavy pear-shaped body on knobby legs; sometimes it stands in the air centimeters above her, sometimes it grips her shoulder in its talons. When the time comes, it will swing its head down savagely as if on a hinge, plummeting like a guillotine, to drive its beak straight through her and kill her.

As in a nightmare, Bellatrix knows it is there but tries, in terror, to ignore it. Still, the terror grows and grows, till she is fevered with it. When the thing like a bird bends louring over her, something like saliva drips from its beak onto her head and arms. She feels it fall, and she shudders but still resists acknowledging it.

Forty years pass in this way.

One never grows accustomed to such terror, but one does eventually tire. The man on the tightrope, if you made him walk it for forty years, would someday gladly fall off.

That is what Bellatrix does: she tires. On the subway home at night, hunched on the seat, when the stuff like saliva begins to drip onto her and she feels the bird's hot breath on her ears, she tires all the way out.

She finally decides, "I just don't care if it kills me."

It is coming. She cannot stop it. "I don't know why it wants to kill me, but I'll *never* know that. I just have to be ready. You're never *ready* ready, but I just—can't stop it."

The long swordlike beak flashes down and gores her. The other people on the subway can't see this, of course; but they do hear the middle-aged woman cry out and see the fount of blood pour from her. People reflexively scramble away. Somebody exclaims, "Bitch got shot!" Somebody panics. Somebody scans outside the windows. Somebody prays to God. Somebody thinks in dreadful anticipation, "Is this it?"

But where is the bird? It is gone.

The Heriot

Nighttime, at home, alone:
"Right now, I'm not hurting anyone"
—a terribly comforting illusion.

When they administer Brad Merle Gost's execution by lethal injection, they will dab his needle wounds with cotton swabs. To prevent infection, presumably.

The last he saw of the world outside was a merciless winter morning years before. It had been the sort of mean, sharp-eyed weather that reminds you that the fix is in, that the ugly-natured racketeers always win, that the weeping innocent still suffer. He has forgotten what day of the week it was.

Brad sits in his cell, waiting for morning. Tapping his foot, without realizing it. Tapping out a slow waltz—the syllables of a name.

A convocation of prisoners crowds into his cell at midnight. Hundreds of them, packed in. Practitioners of automatic writing, inquiring about pardons and paroles in the hereafter. Seeking word from beyond. One of them must have snuck the writing table past the guards. A camera crew appears. A host in a bow tie laughs like a laugher who'd like to be laughing, wipes sweat with a handkerchief, tests his lapel mic. This is just a dry run, people. Cue laugh track. Brad wakes up short of breath. He didn't know he'd fallen asleep.

He blew it big time. His whole life, he puled and schemed and fantasized and double-dealt. Cheating bits of happiness out of life like an unfair transaction fee. Perpetually baleful. Treating unverified hunches like facts from the encyclopedia. Alone everywhere, and everywhere alone.

He had this job as a kid, hauling pianos in a truck with his granddad. They once went out to this housing project, and, as they drove around trying to find the address to deliver to, his granddad told him the story of the guy who'd owned that particular piano before, telling it like it was confidential information, in his low weathered voice. It was a sad story of a man with some dirty secret everybody knew about—that's all Brad recalls of it now. They pulled out of the project and tried to circle back through a shopping arcade, and Brad turned his face up and saw a tall painting of an angel just above the truck window. It was the sign for a bakery.

Morning will come soon. There won't be a pardon. He remembers a particular person. If he could talk to her now, he'd say something like, "I even felt grateful for the folds in your clothes, when you wore them." Though he doesn't really talk like that.

The heavy damp smell outside a bakery. The gradating shadow on a sleeping woman's cheek. Sad, secret stories. Things he can only despair of recalling now. No chance to refresh his memories, nobody to ask. When they used to guillotine people, they'd pick up your head and show you to yourself. Where had he read that?

He'd always been clumsy: he'd never been able to conceal the painfulness of life. Instead he—he did—it. She's dead. Because of his—choice. It's—he still can't face it. He can't say her name. And now the comeuppance. The terror of it crumbles through his flesh, but, when he pays this debt, will it make him not so bad?

He waits for morning in his cell, a scared lost lonely little boy.

Serial Weaponiser

Superstition: reason ungoverned by reason.

Bellatrix rammed the door open with an iron coat stand. It wasn't like the neighbors would hear. She was the only one left on her floor.

She knew where to look. Xin Hui had always kept tinned food in the lower right-hand kitchen cabinet. Everything in the fridge was rotten, and insects had got into the rice. Only the tins were intact. It took Bellatrix two trips to carry them all back to her flat.

It had felt like a dream when the whole world began dying. Bellatrix had barricaded herself into her flat just outside Kuala Lumpur, watching the mobs and riots on TV. Then the plague had gone airborne. The news, while it was still on, had shown people clutching their throats. Twitching long after their hearts had stopped.

Bellatrix put Xin Hui's tins with the rest of her hoard in the spare room. Mackerel in tomato sauce; vegetarian fo tian chiang; maybe pork luncheon meat, though she couldn't read the traditional characters. There was very little Malay or Indian food in Bellatrix's hoard because, as far as she knew, no Malays or Indians had lived in this condominium. There had been lots of condos like that.

She hadn't felt terribly close to her neighbors. She wasn't local, couldn't speak Cantonese. But at least it had been a community. Now it was gone.

Everyone had fled once the dead began to walk. Many had driven north to less populated areas of the peninsula. But the only safety was up high, where the undead would not climb: whenever a band of them began to mount stairs, inexplicably they would tear one another to pieces. From twenty floors up, Bellatrix saw them roaming the parking lots and streets. Sooner or later, she would have to go down.

∽

The stairwell opened from her tower to the pick-up/drop-off area in the avenue in front of the building. Bellatrix stood a few steps above the bottom, out of reach of the undead. Before her, more than a hundred of them milled nearly shoulder to shoulder, swaying and shrieking.

From her window, she'd seen that a small clan of survivors had established quarters in the business hotel across the avenue. She had no idea how she would make it there alive. There were just too many of them.

She heard a scream. A human cry of terror.

From the gap between the hotel and the scuba gear emporium, two human survivors darted out. Both Malays. A petite woman in hijab was in the lead, looking over her shoulder, unaware she was barreling into a gruesome death. The undead in the avenue caught her and, with petrifying squeals, began to rip into her flesh with their teeth.

The heavyset man running behind her, with a crowd of freakishly tall undead stumbling right at his heels, tried to backtrack into the alley. He was too late. The undead in the avenue lunged.

But not at him. They lunged *past* him, swarming over the taller undead and ripping them apart in a feeding frenzy.

The man, in shock at the sight of his companion's death, stood untouched among the pressing horde. And Bellatrix realized something peculiar: From her vantage above the crowd, their heads were all level, nearly geometrically so: none higher, none lower. Likewise the Malay man—he and the undead around him looked exactly the same height. It took Bellatrix a moment to comprehend what she was seeing, but there was no denying it.

Then she saw Xin Hui stumble past. Or what had been Xin Hui. In life, a sprightly and vivacious woman. She and Bellatrix had often shared clothing and laughed over how they were, coincidentally, precisely the same height and dress size.

Bellatrix descended the last few steps and began to weave her way through the shuffling throng. The stench of putrefaction was intense, but the undead simply grunted and stood aside when she brushed against them. She understood now. Among *these* undead, she was safe.

Razbliuto

I say, "This wine is red."
Bellatrix says, "This redness is wine."
We're both wrong.

We're having a video chat.

Your picture is on my screen. It shows you in your chair, in your room in Auckland. You look glad to see me.

But in my room in Andalusia, there's no one in my chair.

In your room in Auckland, there's no one in your chair.

But my picture is on your screen. It shows me in my chair, in my room in Andalusia. I look glad to see you.

Et lux perplexua luceat eis

Your heart is an unopened bill.
You know what you'll find inside.
So there on the sideboard it sits.

I came to the village of Potrastredi shortly before evening on a bracing day in November. The rumours surrounding the village being well known to me, I had resolved a week prior to travel thither and satisfy my curiosity whether the tales were true. But curiosity alone could not account for what drove as much as drew me. The Sácac-Quinaux family fortunes having dwindled nearly away, and all my prior endeavours in both business and belles-lettres coming to wrack, I was desirous of exempting myself from town society; by a paradoxical operation of the heart, the savourlessness of life made of itself a motive, spurring me to flee the familiar.

Discovering, on the outskirts of Potrastredi, an inn which, though in a state of indifferent repair, would serve my purpose for a bed and hot meals, I stabled my horse, then proceeded on foot into the village. The many-storied, steep-roofed houses showed the same evidence of neglect as the inn: slatted shutters hung at angles from bent hinges; patches of missing tile freckled the rooftops; paint peeled from weatherbeaten walls; the gnarled brown remains of flowers long dead drooped forlornly from window planters. It had manifestly been years agone since the denizens had possessed the vigour of life needful to the maintenance of their abodes.

Upon my turning into the square, my senses at once confirmed the truth of all I had heard rumoured. For as many dingy and mournsome-faced villagers walking or loitering on the cobbled square, there were as many, if not more, ghosts.

Villagers prosecuting their daily business were harried at every turn by spectres of varied description. I observed a woman of middle years bearing a sack of flour across the square, behind whom a translucent form, the shade of a youth whose face bore the ravages of pestilence, appeared and snatched a shawl the woman wore against the chill. *'Tis mine*, moaned the youth repeatedly, drawing away from the woman, who gave half-hearted chase with a listlessness as remarkable as the behaviour of her ghostly harasser.

Not far off, a ghost of vengeful mien, in life doubtless an elder of the village, harangued the living most injuriously. *Rot in hell, ye scoundrels! Ye rogues!* A young mother leading two children by the hand shrank from him, lowering her head and hastening past. Another spirit stood near the defunct fountain in the centre of the square and battered herself viciously, beating her own head with her fists so roughly that, more than once, she stumbled and fell.

I resolved to cross the square and enter a public house hard by. Scarcely had I gone a few paces when the shade of a young woman, clad in a tattered, waterlogged wedding dress, materialised before me, sobbing, *I was murthered. He murthered me.* Interest piqued, I attempted to question the ghost, but to each enquiry, be it on the circumstances of her demise, the particulars of her life, or the facts of the world after ours, she only whimpered, *He murthered me.*

With so many spirits afoot even before sundown, I reflected, the nighttime pervasion would indeed be fearsome.

Within the public house, once my eyes had acclimated to the dimness, I found travellers and local Potrastreditans murmuring over flagons of ale at a number of oaken tables as logs smouldered in the hearth. Not a few spirits wandered the floor, passing through walls and furniture; though many a drinker blenched at their approach, none acknowledged their presence. I called for a drink and settled onto a bench beside a man of stoical demeanour.

"You're not from here," he commented. Everyone in this village must have known one another.

A boy thumped a flagon before me as I introduced myself. "Bellatrix Sácac-Quinaux. I am come from the township Borperdi."

"Quite a hike, that. You'll want to move along soon," continued the local man. "As would I, had I the means."

"Your village has—a remarkable ghostly presence." Even as I offered this, a shrill wail filled the public house. I cast my gaze about in alarm. The spectre of a thin, hunched woman flitted betwixt the tables, crying out in terror at every face she met. I heard a man nearby mutter, "Must she yowl ever so?" His companion hushed him, laying her hand on his.

My fellow drinker, when again I faced him, replied, "A presence. Aye, that we have." He tilted his head and darted his eyes to the side. "We've her to thank for that."

I turned to look. In the act of leaving the public house was a sallow woman of middle years, heavily built. "She is?"

"Our gravekeeper."

Having made haste to settle my score, I emerged into the square and, searching for the gravekeeper, spied her vanishing into a small street. I hurried after but was unable to overtake her until she had neared the village graveyard, situated at a remove amidst stretches of swidden. Drawing abreast, I asked without preamble, "Why do so many ghosts walk here?"

It was as though the gravekeeper did not hear me. Only after I had posed my question thrice did she croak, in dialect as archaic as the spirits', "Thou blamest me."

"I wish to know." I took no interest in censuring the woman, though surely the locals laid the onus for the ghostly infestation upon her. All through this land, not excepting my own town, ghosts rose to terrorise the living when bodies were given improper burial. Every township and hamlet had its gravekeeper to see to the rites. When a ghost did rise, a gravekeeper's duty was to exhume and rebury its body with all due honours. Only then would the shade rest.

A filmy rain had begun to fall, and the woman passed a thick, calloused hand over her face. "Blame not where thou knowest not the cause."

Before I could make a rejoinder, in the road appeared the form of a corpulent man in a dressing gown. *Whither goest thou? I like thee not, rind nor pith. What time of day?* The gravekeeper passed directly through him and continued to walk, but I could not bring myself to imitate her. However I manoeuvred, the ghost dogged me, so that I could not get past him; and still his questions and declarations came one on another. *In my youth I went a-soldiering. What trade dost thou profess? 'Twill be a bleak winter.*

By the time I rejoined the gravekeeper, she had attained the graveyard. "Night cometh," she commented. "Thou hadst best get to thine inn." She wended amongst the gravestones, her destination a hut on the far side, and I followed. Seeing I would not be denied an audience, she turned at the entrance to her hovel to regard me, no small impatience evident in her bearing.

"Why do you not put these spirits to rest?" I asked, my tone not hectoring but curious. "Spare these villagers such nightly terror."

The gravekeeper waved her hand as though driving off a gadfly. "Just today did I finish one. Taketh a full week, dost thou know? To exhume and reinter, following all due custom, is not the work of an hour."

"So you are assiduous in your duties?"

The gravekeeper coughed a humourless laugh. "Mayhap God knoweth why I trouble myself, for I know not."

The hair rose at the back of my neck, and I turned involuntarily. Not three paces off stood the shade of a small boy with sable hair, facing me. His eyes did not move, nor the muscles of his face, nor his limbs. In those empty eyes dwelt a power of mesmerism that threatened to palsy my very will.

"Thou art a stranger here." The gravekeeper's harsh voice recalled me to myself, and I turned again to her. "Dost thou know," she continued, "if a gravekeeper herself be not buried with honours, those honours she hath paid to the reburied are sullied withal? Nay, but they become as nought. All ghosts she hath quelled will walk again."

"This I have heard."

"Well, then surely thou hast also heard of the auld custom in these parts: that no gravekeeper may be buried with due honours who hath not finished her work afore she dieth."

This I had not known. But villages in the hinter often maintained ancient practices neglected in the towns. "If you cannot lay all these ghosts to rest, then one day you must join their number."

"'Tis so. As must mine apprentice, and hers in turn." The gravekeeper listlessly waved her fingers as though counting on them. "Dost thou hear? I work without rest, but can only lay in peace half an hundred ghosts in a year."

A few thousand ghosts in a lifetime, I reflected. Surely not an insurmountable number. "How many wander your graveyard?"

For the first time in our interview, the gravekeeper met my eyes directly, turning upon me a gaze as spellbinding as that of the uncanny sable-haired boy I had seen. "Tens of thousands." The despair in her voice seemed to issue from some dry and frigid subterranean cavern, some desolate place with no hope of life. "Tens upon tens of thousands."

She said no further word, but took herself within and eased shut the door. For a moment, I absently regarded this weather-worn door, insensible of the sharpening chill, cognisant only of a qualmishness not unlike that of having stumbled into desecrated ground. When I turned to regard the graveyard that I would be obliged to recross en route to the village and inn, I saw, in the gloaming of the day, ghost after ghost rising to greet the onset of night.

THE THIRTEENTH THIRTEENTH

De cuyo nombre no quiero acordarme

Like a Barefoot Girl Loves the Summer Day

On my way here, all my words fell out.

When you run into Bellatrix Sakakino near Ikenoue Station, you notice she's wearing a T-shirt with very small text printed across the front. Reflexively, your eyes scan it:

If you've ever lost someone close, to a sudden disease or an accident or other calamity, perhaps you've imagined, with heartrending anguish, their dread in the face of the end, the last terrified moment of the blameless.

Or perhaps you've come nigh to losing a loved one, and have envisioned and re-envisioned this in the interval between, say, their initial diagnosis and the eventual relief of learning they would live.

There are those of us who can somehow bear the notion of our own eventual surcease, but who find it unendurable to contemplate the final fearful moments of our dearest companions—a child, a spouse, a bosom friend.

But we all must either watch our loved ones' piteous end, or inflict upon them, by our own departure, the same heartbreak of vicarious deathbed terror.

"Ahem," says Bellatrix, just as you finish reading. "My *eyes* are up here, you know."

Mouthful of Molybdomancy

And yet we remain hopeful about the past.

I haven't been able to finish a song since the day it started. The lyrics just stopped coming.

In the morning, I asked my husband to put new batteries in the kitchen clock. He needed to stand on the piano stool to reach, so he pushed it toward the kitchen with his foot. I swear I'd seen him do it just that way before.

At the supermarket, two middle-aged women in kimono walked past me. One said to the other, in confidential tones, "He ruined himself." Without thinking, I looked around at her and realized I had seen someone in an identically patterned kimono standing in that spot a long time before.

People were collecting money near the crosswalk outside the Marunouchi subway exit. There had been an earthquake, maybe in the Middle East. An older man in a tasteful suit started to argue with a girl at the collection box. I don't know what about. He lost his temper and upset the box. It felt so eerie that I had to sit down.

Three boys were standing in the shadow of a pedestrian bridge. Not talking or moving.

When our son got home, I found out he'd lost his kanji workbook again. Usually he ignores me no matter how I scold him, but this time he burst into tears and ran to his room. I was mystified, so out of character was this for him. And yet—not.

And this evening, in the light of the pachinko parlor entrance, the disconsolate girl sitting and silently crying: Hadn't she been there before?

Geistergarten

I don't exist—I happen.

A daydreamer's story: "I told people he was my lover. I think he worked in a sexy profession. An architect or airline pilot or something. He was tall and Iranian, kept fit, barely spoke, and always had two-day stubble. His only English was, 'I felt like seeing your face.' I'd be out on the veranda, smoking a cigarette. Wondering if maybe today was the end of the world. He'd show up at my apartment without warning. And smile: 'I felt like seeing your face.' We'd take a bath together, at perfect rest."

An infantryman's story: "They sent us up the wrong hill. They filled our guns with the wrong ammunition. They put us under the wrong general. Our boats were pointed in one wrong direction and our planes in another wrong direction. Our flag was the wrong color, blowing the wrong way. We attacked the wrong enemy from the wrong position. I was in the wrong place at the wrong time. You never hear the one that hits you. I leaked, I bubbled, I groaned, I faded. My country... my country... my country wasted me."

An investigator's story: "We couldn't find a next-of-kin. The medical examiner ruled it a cerebral infarction. Her landlord called her a model tenant. The neighbors on her floor were less charitable: 'dirty whore,' 'raunchy bitch,' 'needed a bath'. Still, the case looked commonplace until we searched the house. Found them at the back of the bedroom closet. The desiccated remains, wrapped in plastic, of four stillborn babies. Her diary made no mention of any children. Studied the whole thing, never found a clue. It was just a bleak record of loneliness."

Lebt wohl

Loss is the toll for living.

And what's happening to me?

I found a toenail growing out of my elbow. I plucked a hair from my eyeball. My left hand has become a hoof. My right leg has three joints now. I sneezed out of my ear. I found teeth in my stool. There are gills in my armpits.

All these changes in me—I cannot keep up with them.

Your Torn Frenulum

There is no one she hates more than whoever she was yesterday.

An inn. Two trains, two buses, and a taxi ride through the Niigata mountains. *I never lied. I am only here for one night.* Legs folded on the tatami by the window. Birdsong outside. *But I had one hell of a presentation deck. Gross profit would be such and such. Infrastructure and licenses would cost such and such. Never worked harder on anything. The bank bought it.*

Reaching for the latch, pushing the window open—each movement feels slowed. It takes an hour to settle back onto the floor, or a thousand years. The smell of old tatami. That grassy field smell I don't have a word for. *Seven people trusted me with their careers. Fooled them. Fooled myself. After fifteen years in interior design, who the hell opens a VFX studio?* Outside the window, the countless strains of birdsong blend into a single madrigal. No growling motorbikes or whirring air conditioners. Only tinkling birds. *I should have held those careers in my hands like glass flowers. Cradled them. I thought that's what I was doing, but I—fumbled.* I never learned anything about birds. Was never curious.

Now my slow mind, my slow ears, trace their song. Can't see a single bird outside. The sounds are like fingers squeaking against glass flowers. *We'd joke and call it a "festival" when a project went to hell. All-nighters in the studio. Me ordering pizza for everybody, like I was taking care of them.* I make myself attentive. In the jubilee of leaves and branches, some birds chirrup two notes continuously. Others, trilling runs of five. Some higher, others lower. I have no deeper vocabulary—just "higher," "lower."

I'd known it would be hard, but—god. You trust people, and they find a cheaper solution in Bangkok or Bangalore. Poof. Contract gone. Six months ago, my only interest in this chirping would have been to find patterns. There is no pattern. My slowing mind cradles this notion. *A day comes, you have to tell the team their livelihoods have also gone poof. You see their faces.*

My fault. For fumbling.

To listen is to hear great variety. But each bird has only one song. Another notion occurs to me—that no bird ever thinks of changing its song. All its life, from hatching to death, it'll sing no other. Where did I get this idea? I wonder if it's true, and I blink unforgivable tears from my eyes.

Omissions from the Unsaid

Graced beyond deserving:
Your conscience says to earn it.
Your heart says you cannot.

I heard Bellatrix's familiar thumping footfalls just before she toddled from her bedroom into the kitchen. Even then, I reacted too slowly. As I always did.

"Mommy!" She came in at a near-run, right into my knees—that was her affectionate habit. I ought to have foreseen it. The collision jolted the glass vase from the crook of my arm. Down it fell.

My hands were full with what I'd scooped from the table—books and plates and things—so in that instant I could only watch. The vase nearly grazed her head, landing upended on the tile floor, spilling both flower and water. The rose lost enough petals to warrant throwing out, and, when I picked up the vase, I found a long, straight crack in its mouth.

By then, Bellatrix was back in her room, stifling wretched sobs. I must have shouted.

A Swim in the Glaire

If you did as I do, I'd call you my foe.

The aged stone walls all look the same to you, but you can't be far from the exit. You come to a branch; the way on the right leads to a dead end, so you backtrack, turn left, then choose the right-hand way at the next branch. You run your fingers along the gritty surface of a long curving stretch of wall that leads you rightward, then forces you to double back. The way opens up.

The central chamber. He is there. The minotaur.

Your blood runs backward in terror. Every inch of your skin screams to flee, but your feet are frozen to the floor. The hunched monster turns to face you. Easily twice your height. All rippling muscle. Fierce red eyes. His voice is like distant thunder. "Back again?"

You can do no more than nod.

The minotaur sighs. "Can we talk? Got a minute?" He sits cross-legged on the flagstones. His horns span the opening to the central chamber.

You swallow hard. "Sure." You stand still.

"Come on." He gestures at the floor before him. "It's not like I'm going to eat you or anything."

"Ha, ha." You stay where you are.

He sucks his teeth, shrugs. "Whatever. What a surprise. Nobody likes me anyway." His taurine head droops. "It blows being stuck in here all day."

"You should try to keep busy." You cringe at the banality of your own advice, terrified of saying the wrong thing.

He ignores you. "Lock him up and throw away the key. Out of sight, out of mind. It's totally unfair."

"I'm here now, though." You rush the words out.

"Yeah, great. My savior." He snorts, then shakes his heavy head. "I didn't mean that. I've been under a lot of stress."

"It's fine." You consider sitting down as well, feigning friendship. Perhaps he'll remain calmer. But what if you need to run? You stand poised on the balls of your feet, trembling.

For a while, neither of you speaks. He finally asks, "Are you mad at me?"

"No, of course not. Why?"

"You never come, for one thing." He sounds pettish. "Listen. Hypothetically, okay, say they let me out. What then? I'm a total monster. I'd never get a girlfriend. Forget about a job. No *marketable skills*." He gives the words a bitter twist. "Except for eating people."

You can't help it—your flesh recoils.

"I feel like I literally don't have a future. Because *I* can't change. It's like... like wandering through a night with no moon or stars. I'm so depressed." A long moment passes as the minotaur loses himself in thought. You try to plot an escape. There is only one way back. Left, then right, and right again—then which way was the dead end? You can't remember now. What if you choose wrong?

He breaks the silence. "And I'm always hungry. *Always hungry.*"

Your scalp crawls. "That sounds awful." You stand stock still, but your eyes dart frantically.

In soft, measured syllables, the minotaur says, "I know why you came here." He rises to his feet.

"No reason, really. In fact, I've got to get moving now."

"No."

You giggle. You feel sweat standing on your skin.

"I told you to stay put. Didn't I say that?" He snorts sharply. "You never listen to me. It pisses me off. You hear me?"

"Um."

"It's like the only way I can get you to listen is to make you listen."

"Look, I'm here for you, baby." Will he smell your fear? Can't animals smell fear? "Forever. For as long as you want me."

"It's always me who suffers more. It's always my feelings that are stronger."

"I care for you."

"Prove it one of these days."

It takes all your strength of will not to glance down at his—no, don't think about it. If he were to—ugh. It would kill you. You giggle instead. Not too loud, not too long.

"I know why you came here," he repeats.

If he could not smell your fear before, he must surely smell it now. Every inch of you is clammy, trembling, painfully tense. "You promised you wouldn't eat me."

"Yeah, and you promised to love me."

"I do, baby."

"Your skin is so beautiful."

"I have to go."

"You little bitch."

"For a quick errand. And be right back."

"Shut the fuck up. I know your quick errands. I hear you all the time, sneaking around in the labyrinth. Seeing how close you can get without meeting me. You think I never hear that shit?"

"Come on, baby. That's crazy." Your every nerve strains to flee. You take a short, involuntary step back.

He leans forward, as if he will lunge. But he stands still, breathing out long and angry, lips curling back. "You knew I was here.

De cuyo nombre no quiero acordarme | 173

You came here knowing that. Always here. Always waiting. Always in the dark, alone, sobbing myself to sleep. Always a monster. Always hungry."

"I'll come back. I promise. I just want to go." Your panic peaks. "Please."

"You fucking tease."

"Please let me go home." Tears of terror wet your cheeks.

He raises his heavy head to the sky and bellows. It is louder than anything you could have imagined. The fear this thunderous roar drums into you runs deeper and harder than any fear you have known, rattling through to your very core.

You are certain you will die.

He spits against one of the walls and glares at you, towering over you, eyes full of hatred and rage. "Whatever. Get the fuck out, then." His black spittle drips glutinously down the wall.

You don't dare to move. "I'll be right back."

"See if I care."

"I love you."

"Go."

You back away, feet scuffing the flagstones, kicking pebbles that skitter against the walls. His gaze bores into you. You reach the turning, back past it, whirl around, and run.

Which way? A long curving wall. A switchback. Two lefts, a right. A dead end. Turn. Go back. Turn. Go.

I know why you came here. His voice, from behind. No. A memory. You run faster.

That is not his breath on your neck. That is your imagination.

I love you. You told him this only because you had to. Run. Turn left. *I came to see you.* This was a lie. Go left again. Not true.

Another right turn, and the way doubles back. You've seen this turning before. The exit must be near.

The parabolist is indebted to all who have offered words of encouragement for and criticism of these parables, most notably Bethany M. Wenner, whose ideas and support have been invaluable.

∾

Many thanks also to the editors and staff at the magazines which first published many of these parables. Publication acknowledgements appear in the *Schedule of Parables* overleaf.

Schedule of Parables

AUTUMN ON VENUS

Dree Your Weird ... 4
First published in ThereAfter Magazine no. 1.

Albumen Skyline ... 5

Ngantukisme ... 7
First published in New World Writing.

Et sic per gradus ad ima tenditur ... 8
Edited by Maya Sabatino for Pep Haus.
Content warning: *mention of death.*

A New Lease on Life (with No Escape Clause) ... 11
First published in Bright Flash Literary Review.

White Hat Bias ... 13
Content warning: *a fatal traffic accident.*

The Martyr's Palm ... 15
First published in Rue Scribe.

BURGLAR'S WINE

We Drink Pearls—We Sup on Peacocks' Tongues ... 18
First published under the title "If You Needed It, You'd Be Dead by Now" in Riggwelter no. 27.

Þanne Ytemeste Ferþyng ... 19
Content warning: *death.*

Endlessly Cutting the Deck ... 21

Excellent Problem-Causing and Critical-Drinking Skills ... 23
Content warning: *description of torture.*

It Is One Hundred Years since Our Children Left ... 24
First published in Impossible Task no. 8.
Content warning: *food and illness.*

Life with Good Demons ... 25

My Teeth Floated Out of My Mouth ... 26

CHEWING YOUR CREMAINS

Tumpangisme ... 30
First published in Vol.1 Brooklyn.

Holocutor ... 32

Privatspheric Pressure ... 33

Se Unclæna Gast ... 34

Insolubilia	35
Farewell to the Anthropocene	36
Disconcordance	37

PUNCHLINE TO THE APOCALYPSE

Brain, Brain, Go Away	40
Dryshod on the Waterface	41
Gardener of Human Happiness First published in After Dinner Conversation. **Content warning:** mention of execution.	43
Burning of Judas First published in Twin Pies Literary vol. IV.	44
Persona bajo la lluvia	46
Droll Tin Pannikins **Content warning:** thematic hint of fat-shaming.	48
Eia, wärn wir da!	49

GOOD MORNING TURNKEY

Fortnight of New Moons **Content warning:** allusion to suicide.	52
My Memoirs Won't Mention You **Content warning:** dead body parts.	53
Murmurs in the Moiré First published in Press Pause vol. 4.	55
Whilst This Machine Is to Him First published in After Dinner Conversation. **Content warning:** severed body parts.	57
What Average Opinion Expects Average Opinion to Be	59
Lies Breathed Through Silver First published in Gone Lawn no. 39. **Content warning:** mention of broken bones.	62
World Turns to Slurry First published in Fudoki Magazine. **Content warning:** allusion to suicide.	64

BEWARE THE ROPE'S END

Obstrepolice	68
Care for a Canoodle? First published in The Daily Drunk.	69
Welcome and Heeded Prophets	71

Tant pis	72
Content warning: *reference to bullying.*	
Whatever Will Bain't, Will Bain't	73
Content warning: *mention of death and blood.*	
Amorous Echolalia	75
Motif f388	76

LEARNÈD HELPLESSNESS

Tip of the Icepick	78
Verbigeration	79
Virus sin nombre	80
First published in The Red Lemon Review no. 1.	
Content warning: *hints of mental illness.*	
Native Adjectising	82
First published under the title "Firstable" in The Molotov Cocktail vol. 11 no. 10.	
Creeping Infallibility	84
First published in The Avenue no. 7.	
Squelette articulé	85
A Purloined Hitherside	87

THE HECKLER'S VETO

Pontengisme	92
First published in The Collidescope.	
Content warning: *a misogynistic slur.*	
You've Got Ruin Value	95
Spillikins	96
Content warning: *heart failure and a fatal shooting.*	
Lives Forgone in Worlds Fantastical	98
Content warning: *mention of illness, death, cancer, and abortion.*	
You Put the Speck in Speculation	99
First published in Fever Dream Journal.	
Nyetovshchik	101
First published in Defenestration.	
Antapocatastatic Peace	102

BUREAUCRACIDE

My Memoirs Won't Mention Me	104
First published in Sonder Midwest.	
Content warning: *fatal shootings.*	

Antediluvian Optimism · 106
First published in Sci-Fi Lampoon winter 2021 ed.
Content warning: *a person is devoured by an animal.*

Faute de mieux · 108
First published in Toyon Literary Magazine vol. 67.

Geomancing the Stone · 110

Faitiche · 112

Cancellist · 113

Á sjálf sig þau trûðu · 114
First published in After Dinner Conversation.
Content warning: *mention of illness and death.*

YOUR RUINED SEPTUM

Manywhere · 118
First published in pacificREVIEW.
Content warning: *thematic hint of incest.*

Nam deteriores omnes sumus licentiæ · 121

Stepping Gingerly · 122
Content warning: *a maiming accident.*

Desengaños del mundo · 123
Content warning: *cannibalism.*

maltnalt your grlp · 124
Content warning: *thematic hint of fat-shaming.*

Bumptious Billingsgate · 125

Filemot · 127

CONTREVOYANT DREAMS

Un poco alterado · 130
First published under the title "Tints and Hues" in Short Circuit no. 8, Short Édition's quarterly review.

Read 'Em, Wept · 132
Content warning: *ableist and misogynistic slurs.*

Retroactive Discontinuity · 133
First published in The Avenue no. 7.
Content warning: *an incident of sexual harassment.*

On donne l'idée du vrai avec du faux · 135
First published in Menacing Hedge no. 10.03.

Ignormal · 138

Tayy al-Arḍ · 139
First published in MoonPark Review no. 15.

Unring the Bells	140
First published in Masque & Spectacle no. 22.	
Content warning: *mention of death.*	

VARIED PARALYSES

Done and Dusted	144
First published in Masque & Spectacle no. 22.	
Content warning: *death.*	
Pass the Freedom Fries	146
Dysregulation	147
First published in Wrongdoing Magazine no. 1.	
Content warning: *violent death and a misogynistic slur.*	
The Heriot	149
First published in Punk Noir Magazine.	
Content warning: *allusion to murder.*	
Serial Weaponiser	151
First published under the title "We Shared Clothing and Laughed" in Bowery Gothic.	
Content warning: *illness and violent death.*	
Razbliuto	154
Et lux perplexua luceat eis	155
First published in Grim & Gilded no. 3.	
Content warning: *mention of death and murder.*	

DE CUYO NOMBRE NO QUIERO ACORDARME

Like a Barefoot Girl Loves the Summer Day	162
Content warning: *mention of death.*	
Mouthful of Molybdomancy	163
First published in New World Writing.	
Geistergarten	165
First published in Bluepepper.	
Content warning: *violent death, misogynistic slurs, and stillbirth.*	
Lebt wohl	167
Your Torn Frenulum	168
Omissions from the Unsaid	170
First published in CP Quarterly no. 10.	
A Swim in the Glaire	171
An early version was first published in Rue Scribe.	
Content warning: *implied threat of sexual violence.*	

Printed in Great Britain
by Amazon